The Inspector General

Dover Thrift Editions

Nikolai Gogol

Translated by
John Laurence Seymour
and George Rapall Noyes

Dover Publications
Garden City, New York

DOVER THRIFT EDITIONS
GENERAL EDITOR: STANLEY APPELBAUM
EDITOR OF THIS VOLUME: THOMAS CROFTS

Copyright

Bibliographical Note

This Dover edition, first published in 1995, reprints the translation originally appearing (as *The Inspector*) in *Masterpieces of the Russian Drama*, George Rapall Noyes, ed., D. Appleton and Company, New York, in 1933, and subsequently republished in two volumes by Dover, by special arrangement with Harvard University, in 1960.

Library of Congress Cataloging-in-Publication Data

Gogol', Nikolaĭ Vasil'evich, 1809–1852.
[Revizor. English]
The Inspector General / Nikolai Gogol ; translated by John Laurence Seymour and George Rapall Noyes.
p. cm.
Originally published: The Inspector, in Masterpieces of the Russian Drama, New York : D. Appleton, 1933.
ISBN-13: 978-0-486-28500-9
ISBN-10: 0-486-28500-6
I. Seymour, John Laurence. II. Noyes, George Rapall, 1873–1952. III. Title.
PG3333.R4 1995
891.73'3—dc20 94-23925
CIP

Manufactured in the United States of America
28500609 2021
www.doverpublications.com

Note

Nikolai Vasilyevich Gogol (1809–1852) had his first literary success with *Evenings on a Farm near Dikanka* (1831–1832), a group of tales set in the author's native Ukrainian countryside and portraying expressively the language and traditions of the region's Cossacks. In these and subsequent stories, Gogol both satirized and memorialized the proclivities of rural Russians and St. Petersburg bureaucrats.

The Inspector General (1836) is a devilish satire on the corruption of the Russian government's minor officialdom. Portrayed are a group of small-town officials, headed by the voluble and high-strung Chief of Police, who are as delightfully funny as they are wholly devoid of principles. Hilarious though it is, the play was a scorching (and daring) indictment of the state of the Russian government under Tsar Nicholas I. The beautifully simple plot and exquisitely caustic humor of *The Inspector General* indeed had the effect of a well-placed explosive. When produced in 1836 (with the special permission of the tsar) it polarized literate Russia, and, though befriended by some of the greatest Russian writers of the day, including Alexander Pushkin, Sergey Asakov and the critic Vissarion Belinksy, Gogol encountered such hostility from his detractors (most of them the victims of his satire) that he fled to Rome and there remained until 1842. (He returned to Russia in that year with the manuscript of his second masterpiece, the novel *Dead Souls*.)

Included in this edition are Gogol's own "Notes for the Actors," providing guidance in the stage portrayal of the characters, and well as an invaluable fleshing out of the chief participants in the remarkable episodes that follow.

Note: Throughout, footnotes carry the attribution "Sykes" or "Adapted from Sykes." The reference is to Arthur A. Sykes, an early translator of the play (1892) whose notes were retained by the previous editor Noyes, whose own footnotes also appear in the present edition.

CHARACTERS *

Antón Antónovich Skvóznik-Dmukhanóvsky, *chief of police*
Anna Andréyevna, *his wife*
Márya Antónovna, *his daughter*
Luká Lúkich Hlópov, *superintendent of schools*
His Wife
Ammós Fédorovich Lyápkin-Tyápkin, *judge*
Artémy Filíppovich Zemlyaníka, *supervisor of charitable institutions*
Iván Kúzmich Shpékin, *postmaster*
Petr Ivánovich Dóbchinsky
Petr Ivánovich Bóbchinsky
} *landed proprietors living in the town*
Iván Alexándrovich Hlestakóv, *an official from St. Petersburg*
Osip, *his servant*
Christián Ivánovich Gíbner, *district physician*
Fédor Andréyevich Lyulyukóv
Iván Lazarévich Rastakóvsky
Stepán Ivánovich Koróbkin
} *retired officials, respected personages in the town*
Stepán Ilyích Ukhovértov, *police captain*
Svistunóv
Púgovitsyn
Derzhímorda
} *policemen*
Abdúlin, *a merchant*
Fevrónya Petróva Poshlépkin, *wife of a locksmith*
Widow *of a* Sergeant
Míshka, *servant of the chief of police*
Inn Servant
Men and women guests, merchants, townsfolk, petitioners.

---

* Several of these names have grotesque associations; the following translations may serve: Skvoznik-Dmukhanovsky, Rascal-Puftup; Hlopov, Bedbug; Lyapkin-Tyapkin, Bungle-Steal; Zemlyanika, Strawberry; Hlestakov, Whippersnapper; Lyulyukov, Halloo; Rastakovsky, Sayyes; Korobkin, Woodenhead; Ukhovertov, Earwig; Svistunov, Whistle; Pugovitsyn, Buttons; Derzhimorda, Holdyourmug; Abdulin, Tatar; Poshlepkin (pronounced Po-shlyop'kin), Draggletail. Fedor is pronounced Fyŏ'dor; Fedorovich, Fyŏ'do-ro-vich; Shpekin, Shpyŏ'kin; Ukhovterov, U-kho-vyŏr'toff; Petr, Pyŏtr (one syllable).

CHARACTERS AND COSTUMES

NOTES FOR THE ACTORS

The CHIEF OF POLICE * has grown old in the service and is, in his own way, anything but a stupid man. Although a bribe-taker, he behaves with marked dignity; he is rather serious, and is even somewhat inclined to moralize; he speaks neither loudly nor softly, much nor little. His every word is significant. His features are harsh and coarse, such as are common in people who have advanced with difficulty from the lowest ranks. The change from fear to joy, from servility to arrogance, is very sudden, as in the case of a man with crudely developed personal traits. He is dressed in the usual manner, in his uniform with frogs, wearing high boots with spurs. His hair is cut short and shows gray streaks.

ANNA ANDREYEVNA, his wife, is a provincial coquette, still in middle life, brought up half on novels and albums, half on bustling about her housekeeping supplies and supervising her maids. She is very inquisitive, and on occasion displays vanity. Sometimes she gets the upper hand of her husband simply because he is unable to answer her, but this power extends only to trifles and consists of curtain lectures and nagging. During the course of the play she changes her costume four times.

HLESTAKOV is a young man twenty-three years old, very thin and lean; he is rather stupid, and, as they say, rattle-headed, one of those people who in their offices are called hopelessly "dumb." He speaks and acts without any reflection. He is incapable of focusing his attention on any thought whatsoever. His speech is abrupt, and the words fly out of his mouth quite unexpectedly. The more sincerity and simplicity the actor puts into this rôle, the better he will play it. He is dressed fashionably.

OSIP is the usual sort of elderly manservant. He talks seriously, and has a rather condescending air; he is inclined to moralize, and likes to sermonize his master behind his back. His voice is almost unchang-

* The office of *gorodnichy*, or chief of city police, existed from 1775 to 1862. The *gorodnichy* was appointed by the imperial authorities in St. Petersburg and was responsible to them. His duties were far more extensive than those of the chief of police of an American or an English city. The title *city manager* might suggest them more accurately.

ing: in conversation with his master he assumes a severe, abrupt, and even rather rude expression. He is cleverer than his master, and therefore grasps a situation more quickly; but he does not like to talk much, and is a silent rascal. He wears a gray or blue frock coat, much worn.

BOBCHINSKY and DOBCHINSKY are both short and stubby and very inquisitive, extraordinarily like each other: both are slightly corpulent; both speak very fast with an extraordinary amount of gesticulation. Dobchinsky is a little taller and more serious than Bobchinsky, but Bobchinsky is more expansive and lively than Dobchinsky.

LYAPKIN-TYAPKIN, the Judge, is a man who has read five or six books, and is consequently something of a freethinker. He is very fond of conjectures, and therefore gives much weight to his every word. The actor who plays the rôle must always preserve a knowing expression of countenance. He speaks in a bass voice with a prolonged drawl, with a sound of wheezing and strangling, like an old clock, which first squeaks and then strikes.

ZEMLYANIKA, the Supervisor of Charitable Institutions, is a very stout, awkward, and clumsy man, but for all that a schemer and a rogue. He is very officious and bustling.

THE POSTMASTER is simple-hearted to the point of naïveté.

The remaining rôles require no special explanations: their prototypes may be found in almost any community.

The actors should pay particular attention to the last scene. The last speech should produce upon all a sudden electric shock. The whole group should strike its pose in a twinkling. A cry of astonishment should be uttered by all the women at once, as if proceeding from a single bosom. From a disregard of these remarks may result a total loss of effect.

Don't blame the looking-glass if your mug is crooked.

POPULAR PROVERB

ACT I

A room in the house of the CHIEF OF POLICE

SCENE I

CHIEF OF POLICE, SUPERVISOR OF CHARITABLE INSTITUTIONS, SUPERINTENDENT OF SCHOOLS, JUDGE, POLICE CAPTAIN, DISTRICT PHYSICIAN, *and two* SERGEANTS OF POLICE

CHIEF OF POLICE: I have invited you here, gentlemen, in order to communicate to you a most unpleasant piece of news: a government inspector is coming to visit us.

AMMOS FEDOROVICH: What, an inspector?

ARTEMY FILIPPOVICH: What, an inspector?

CHIEF OF POLICE: An inspector from Petersburg, incognito. And furthermore, with secret instructions.

AMMOS FEDOROVICH: Well, I declare!

ARTEMY FILIPPOVICH: As if we didn't have troubles enough already!

LUKA LUKICH: Oh, my God, and with secret instructions too!

CHIEF OF POLICE: I had a sort of presentiment. All last night I kept dreaming about two most extraordinary rats. Honest, I've never seen any like them: black, and awfully big. They came, sniffled about, and went away again. And now I'm going to read you a letter that I've received from Andrey Ivanovich Chmykhov, whom you know, Artemy Filippovich. Here's what he writes: "My dear friend, godfather, and benefactor," (*He mutters in an undertone, rapidly glancing over the letter.*) . . . "and to inform you." Ah, here it is! "I hasten to inform you, by the way, that an official has arrived with instructions to inspect the whole province and especially our district. (*Raising his fingers significantly.*) I have found this out from most reliable people, although he is representing himself as a private individual. Knowing as I do that you, like everybody else, are liable to your little failings, because you're a smart chap and don't like to miss anything that fairly swims into your hands . . ." (*After a pause.*) Well, this is a friendly party. . . . "I advise you to take precautions, because he may arrive at any moment, if he hasn't already, and isn't living somewhere around now, incognito. . . . Yesterday I . . ." Well, next there's some family matters: "Cousin Anna Kirilovna has come to see us with her husband; Ivan Kirilovich has grown very stout, and he plays on the fiddle all the time . . ." and so forth, and so on. Now there's a fix for you!

AMMOS FEDOROVICH: Yes, and such an unusual fix; absolutely extraordinary! There's something up.

LUKA LUKICH: But why on earth, Anton Antonovich; what's this for? Why send an inspector here?

CHIEF OF POLICE: What for? Evidently it's fate. (*Sighing.*) Up to this time, thanks be to God, they've poked into other people's business; but now it's our turn.

AMMOS FEDOROVICH: I think, Anton Antonovich, that in this case it's for a subtle and more political reason. Here's what it means: Russia . . . yes . . . Russia's going to war; and the ministry, you see, has sent the official to find out if there's any treason brewing.

CHIEF OF POLICE: Where do you get that stuff? Aren't you the smart man! Treason in a provincial town! Is this a frontier town? Why, you can gallop away from here for three years without reaching a foreign country.

AMMOS FEDOROVICH: No, I tell you, you don't understand . . . you don't . . . The authorities have subtle ideas: even if it is a long distance, they aren't taking any chances.

CHIEF OF POLICE: Whether they are or not, gentlemen, I've warned you. See here: I've made, for my part, some kind of arrangements, and I advise you to do the same. Especially you, Artemy Filippovich! No doubt the passing official will want first of all to inspect the charitable institutions belonging to your department, and therefore you'd better see that everything's in decent shape: the nightcaps had better be clean, and the patients had better not look like blacksmiths, as they usually do, in their little home circle.

ARTEMY FILIPPOVICH: Come, that's all right. They can put on clean nightcaps if you want.

CHIEF OF POLICE: Yes. And also above each bed write up in Latin or some such language—here, that's your job, Christian Ivanovich—the name of each disease, when the person was taken ill, and the day of the week and month. . . . And it's a bad thing that your patients smoke such strong tobacco that a fellow always begins to sneeze as soon as he goes in. Yes, and it would be better if there were fewer of 'em: people will attribute it right off to bad supervision or to the doctor's lack of skill.

ARTEMY FILIPPOVICH: Oh, so far as the doctoring goes, Christian Ivanovich and I have taken our measures: the closer you get to nature, the better; we don't use expensive medicines. Man's a simple creature: if he's going to die, he dies; if he's going to get well, he gets well. And besides it would be hard for Christian Ivanovich to consult with them: he doesn't know a word of Russian.

(CHRISTIAN IVANOVICH *utters a sound somewhat like the letter "e" and a little like "a."*)

CHIEF OF POLICE: I'd also advise you, Ammos Fedorovich, to pay some attention to the courthouse. There in the hall where the petitioners usually appear, the janitors have started raising domestic geese and goslings, and they all duck under your feet as you walk. Of course it's praiseworthy for every man to look after his domestic enterprises, and why shouldn't a janitor? Only in such a place, you know, it's hardly suitable. . . . I meant to bring that to your attention before, but somehow I forgot it.

AMMOS FEDOROVICH: Well, I'll order them all taken away to my kitchen this very day. Come to dinner if you want to.

CHIEF OF POLICE: Besides that it's a bad thing that you have all kinds of rubbish drying up right in the court room, and a hunter's whip right over the cupboard where the documents are kept. I know that you like hunting, but all the same you'd better remove it for a while; and then, when the government inspector has gone away, you can hang it up there again. And your assessor likewise . . . of course, he's a well-informed man, but he smells exactly as if he'd just come out of a distillery—and that's no good either. I've been going to speak to you about that for some time back; but I was distracted, I don't remember how. There's a remedy against that smell, if, as he says, it's actually natural to him: he can be advised to eat onions or garlic or something else. In that case Christian Ivanovich might help out with some drugs.

(CHRISTIAN IVANOVICH *utters the same sound.*)

AMMOS FEDOROVICH: No, it's impossible to drive it out. He says that in his childhood his nurse bumped him and that since that time he smells a little of vodka.

CHIEF OF POLICE: Well, I only brought it to your notice. So far as internal arrangements go and what Andrey Ivanovich calls in his letter little failings, I can't say anything, and it would be queer to talk about them, for there's no man who hasn't some weaknesses or other. Why, God himself has fixed it like that, and the Voltairians make a great mistake to say anything to the contrary.

AMMOS FEDOROVICH: And what do you presume to call failings, Anton Antonovich? There are sins and sins. I tell everybody openly that I take bribes—but what kind of bribes? Wolfhound puppies. That's absolutely another matter.

CHIEF OF POLICE: Well, puppies or anything else—it's bribes, all the same.

AMMOS FEDOROVICH: Indeed not, Anton Antonovich. Here, for instance, if a man accepts a fur coat worth five hundred rubles, or a shawl for his wife . . .

CHIEF OF POLICE: Well, and what if you do accept only wolfhound puppies as bribes? To make up for it, you don't believe in God; you never go to church; but I am at least firm in the faith, and I go to church every Sunday. But you . . . Oh, I know you: if you begin to talk about the creation of the world, my hair simply stands on end.

AMMOS FEDOROVICH: But you see I reasoned it out for myself, with my own intellect.

CHIEF OF POLICE: Well, in some cases it's worse to have too much intellect than to have none at all. However, I merely wanted to mention the district court; but to tell the truth, I doubt that any one will ever take a peep at it; it's such an enviable place, God Himself must protect it. Now, as for you, Luka Lukich, as supervisor of educational institutions, you'd better take special care of the teachers. Of course they're learned people, educated in various colleges; but they have very strange ways, naturally inseparable from their learned calling. One of them, for instance, the one with the fat face . . . I don't remember his name . . . when he gets on the platform can't do without making faces, like this (*making a grimace*) and then begins to iron out his beard with his hand, from under his cravat. Of course, when he pulls a snout like that at one of the pupils, it doesn't matter much, and it may even be necessary for all I can say; but judge for yourself if he should do it to a visitor—that would be awful: the government inspector or whoever it was might consider it personal, and the devil knows what might come of it.

LUKA LUKICH: Surely, but what can I do with him? I've spoken to him about it several times already. Here, just a few days ago, when our marshal of nobility happened to drop in on the class, he cut such a mug as I've never seen before. Of course he did it with the best heart in the world, but I got called down: "Why," says they, "are our young people being exposed to the contagion of freethinking?"

CHIEF OF POLICE: I ought also to mention your history teacher. His head's full of learning, that's evident, and he's picked up information by the ton; only he gets so hot in his explanations that there's no understanding him. I once listened to him: well, while he was talking about the Assyrians and the Babylonians, it was all right; but when he got as far as Alexander of Macedon I can't tell you what came over him. Damme if I didn't think there was a fire! He ran down from the platform, and banged a chair against the door with all his might.

Of course, Alexander of Macedon was a hero; but why smash the chairs over him? It causes a loss to the treasury.

LUKA LUKICH: Yes, he's hot-headed. I've remarked the fact to him several times already. . . . He says, "Just as you please: for science I won't spare life itself."

CHIEF OF POLICE: Yes, such is the inexplicable law of the Fates: a wise man is either a drunkard or he makes such faces that you've got to carry out the holy ikons.*

LUKA LUKICH: God save us from serving in the educational line! A fellow's afraid of everybody: all sorts of people interfere, and they all want to show that they're educated, too.

CHIEF OF POLICE: But all this wouldn't amount to anything—it's that damned incognito! He'll look in all of a sudden with an "Oh, here you are, sweethearts! And who's the judge here?" he'll say.—"Lyapkin-Tyapkin."—"All right, hand over Lyapkin-Tyapkin! And who's the supervisor of charitable institutions?"—"Zemlyanika."—"Well, hand over Zemlyanika!"—That's what's bad!

SCENE II

The same and the POSTMASTER

POSTMASTER: Will you explain, gentlemen, what sort of official is coming, and why?

CHIEF OF POLICE: But haven't you heard?

POSTMASTER: I heard something from Petr Ivanovich Bobchinsky. He just called on me at the post office.

CHIEF OF POLICE: Well, then, what do you think about it?

POSTMASTER: What do I think? I think we're going to war with the Turks.

AMMOS FEDOROVICH: Right-o! That's exactly what I thought.

CHIEF OF POLICE: Yes, but you're both talking through your hat!

POSTMASTER: Sure, it's war with the Turks. The French keep spoiling everything.

CHIEF OF POLICE: War with the Turks, your grandmother! *We're* going to be in a mess, not the Turks. We know that already; I have a letter.

POSTMASTER: If that's so, then there's not going to be war with the Turks.

CHIEF OF POLICE: Well, then, how about you, Ivan Kuzmich?

POSTMASTER: About me? How about you, Anton Antonovich?

CHIEF OF POLICE: Well, what about me? I'm not afraid: that is,

* "To avoid shocking them."—Sykes.

only a little. . . . The merchants and the townspeople make me uneasy. They say that I'm somewhat hard-boiled; but if I've ever taken anything from anybody, God knows it was without the least ill-feeling. I even think (*taking him by the arm and leading him aside*), I even think there may have been some private denunciation of me. Otherwise why in the world send the inspector to us? Now listen here, Ivan Kuzmich, hadn't you better, for our mutual benefit just unseal and read every letter that arrives at the post office, both incoming and outgoing? You know, just in case there should be some sort of denunciation, or simply, correspondence. If there isn't, of course you can seal them up again; or, so far as that goes, you can even deliver them opened.

POSTMASTER: I know, I know. . . . Don't try to teach me. I do it already, not as a precaution, but more out of curiosity; I'm deadly fond of finding out what's new in the world. I tell you, it's most interesting reading. There are piles of letters that you'll thoroughly enjoy, certain passages are so descriptive . . . and they're so instructive . . . lots better than the *Moscow News*.

CHIEF OF POLICE: Well, tell me, haven't you ever come across anything about some such official from Petersburg?

POSTMASTER: No, absolutely nothing about any one from Petersburg, but there's a lot said about those from Kostroma and Saratov. However, it's a pity that *you* don't read the letters: there are some corking places in them. Not long ago a lieutenant was writing to a friend and he described a ball in the most playful way . . . it was awfully good: "My life, my dear friend, is being passed in the empyrean," he says; "there are lots of young ladies; the band is playing; the standard gallops by. . . ." He described it all with very great feeling. I kept the letter out just on purpose. Do you want me to read it to you?

CHIEF OF POLICE: Well, this is hardly the time for it. So you'll do me the favor, Ivan Kuzmich, if you accidentally come across a complaint or a denunciation, to keep it back without any question.

POSTMASTER: With the greatest of pleasure.

AMMOS FEDOROVICH: Look out, or you'll catch it for that, sometime!

POSTMASTER: Great Scott!

CHIEF OF POLICE: Never mind, never mind. It would be another story if you were to make anything public out of it; but you see, this is a family matter.

AMMOS FEDOROVICH: Yes, a nasty mess has been brewed! I admit I was going to call on you, Anton Antonovich, to make you a present of a little bitch. She's a sister to the dog you know. You've doubtless heard that Cheptovich and Varkhovinsky have started a lawsuit, so that now I'm living in luxury: I course hares now on one man's land, now on the other's.

CHIEF OF POLICE: Holy Saints, I don't care anything about your hares now! I can't get that damned incognito out of my head. You wait until the door opens, and then suddenly—

SCENE III

The same, with DOBCHINSKY *and* BOBCHINSKY, *who both come in panting*

BOBCHINSKY: An extraordinary event!

DOBCHINSKY: What unexpected news!

ALL: Why, what is it?

DOBCHINSKY: A most unforeseen affair. We went into the inn—

BOBCHINSKY (*interrupting*): Petr Ivanovich and I went into the inn—

DOBCHINSKY (*interrupting*): Hey, if you please, Petr Ivanovich, I'll tell it!

BOBCHINSKY: Hey yourself, let me . . . let me, let me . . . you haven't got the right style. . . .

DOBCHINSKY: But you'll get all balled up and won't remember everything.

BOBCHINSKY: I'll remember, by George, I'll remember! Only don't mix in, let me tell it; don't meddle! Gentlemen, please tell Petr Ivanovich not to interfere!

CHIEF OF POLICE: Yes, for God's sake, tell us what's up! My heart's in my mouth. Be seated, gentlemen; take chairs! Petr Ivanovich, here's a chair for you. (*All seat themselves around the two* PETR IVANOVICHES.) Well now, what's up?

BOBCHINSKY: Allow me, allow me; I'll tell everything in order. No sooner had I had the pleasure of leaving you after you had got all upset over the receipt of that letter—yes, sir—than I just dropped in . . . now, please don't interrupt, Petr Ivanovich! I already know all, all, all about it, sir! So, as you'll be kind enough to see, I dropped in on Korobkin. But not finding Korobkin at home, I turned in at Rastakovsky's; and not finding Rastakovsky, I went straight to Ivan Kuzmich in order to communicate to him the news you had received; and then, going away from there, I met Petr Ivanovich—

DOBCHINSKY (*interrupting*): Near the stall where they sell meat pies.

BOBCHINSKY: Near the stall where they sell meat pies. Yes, I met up with Petr Ivanovich; and I said to him, "Have you heard the news that Anton Antonovich has received in a trustworthy letter?" But Petr Ivanovich had already heard about it from your housekeeper, Avdotya, who had been sent, I don't know what for, to Filipp Antonovich Pochechuyev's.

DOBCHINSHY (*interrupting*): For a little keg for French brandy.

BOBCHINSKY (*pushing his hands aside*): For a little keg for French brandy. So Petr Ivanovich and I went to Pochechuyev's. . . . For heaven's sake, Petr Ivanovich, don't interrupt; please don't interrupt! . . . We went to Pochechuyev's, and on the way Petr Ivanovich said to me: "Let's stop," he says, "at the inn. I haven't had anything in my stomach since morning, and it's simply flopping about. . . ." Yes, sir, Petr Ivanovich's belly was. . . . "But they've just brought some fresh salmon into the inn," he says, "and we'll take a snack." Well, no sooner were we in the hotel, when suddenly a young man—

DOBCHINSKY (*interrupting*): Not bad-looking, in civilian clothes. . . .

BOBCHINSKY: Not bad-looking, in civilian clothes, was walking up and down the room with such a thoughtful expression on his face and in his actions, and here (*putting his hand over his forehead*) much of everything, very much. I had a sort of presentiment, and I says to Petr Ivanovich: "There's more in this than meets the eye." Yes, I did. But Petr Ivanovich beckoned to me with his finger and we called the innkeeper, sir, the innkeeper Vlas. His wife was confined three weeks ago; and such a smart boy, too, he's going to take care of the inn just like his daddy. Well, having called Vlas, Petr Ivanovich asked him on the quiet: "Who's that young man?" he says. And Vlas answered, "Why that . . ." Hey, don't interrupt, Petr Ivanovich; please don't interrupt; you won't be able to tell it, God knows you won't: you lisp. I know you've got a tooth in your head that whistles. . . . "That young man," he says, "is an official." Yes, sir. "He's come from Petersburg," says Vlas, "and his name is Ivan Alexandrovich Hlestakov, sir; and he's going," says Vlas, "into the Province of Saratov; and," he says, "he's certainly acting queer: this is the second week he's been here, he never goes outside of the tavern; he orders everything on account; and he won't pay a kopek." As soon as he had told me that, I saw through it at once. "Aha!" I said to Petr Ivanovich—

DOBCHINSKY: No, Petr Ivanovich, it was I who said "Aha!"

BOBCHINSKY: You said it first, but I said it next. "Aha!" said Petr Ivanovich and I. "But why has he come here if he's headed for the Province of Saratov?"—Yes, sir. And so he must be that official.

CHIEF OF POLICE: Who? What official?

BOBCHINSKY: Why, that there official that you received the notice about, the government inspector.

CHIEF OF POLICE (*frightened*): What the deuce are you saying? That can't be he!

DOBCHINSKY: Yes, it is! He doesn't pay and he doesn't go. How could it be anybody else? And his traveling papers are made out for Saratov.

BOBCHINSKY: It's he; it's he, by God, it's he. . . . And what an observing fellow: he inspected everything. He even noticed that Petr Ivanovich and I were eating salmon, chiefly because Petr Ivanovich, on account of his stomach . . . well, yes, he even took a look in our plates. I fairly shivered with fright.

CHIEF OF POLICE: O Lord, forgive us sinners! Where's he staying?

DOBCHINSKY: In number five, under the staircase.

BOBCHINSKY: In the very same room where those traveling officers had a fight last year.

CHIEF OF POLICE: Has he been here long?

DOBCHINSKY: Just two weeks. He came on the day of St. Vasily of Egypt.

CHIEF OF POLICE: Two weeks! (*Aside.*) Holy Saints and Martyrs, get us out of this! In these two weeks the sergeant's wife has been beaten up! No provisions have been issued to the prisoners! The streets are like a dramshop, such filth! Oh, shame! Disgrace! (*He clutches at his head.*)

ARTEMY FILIPPOVICH: What do you think, Anton Antonovich: shall we go in a body to the hotel?

AMMOS FEDOROVICH: No, no! Let the Chief of Police go first, then the clergy, and the merchants—isn't that the way it is in the book, *The Deeds of John the Mason*? *

CHIEF OF POLICE: No, no, please leave it to me. Difficult situations have occurred in my life, but they have turned out all right, and I have even been thanked. Maybe God will get us off this time. (*Turning to* BOBCHINSKY.) You say he's a young man?

BOBCHINSKY: He is; not much over twenty-three or four.

CHIEF OF POLICE: All the better: you can smell out a young one quicker. It's fierce when it's an old devil; but a young one is all on the surface. Get your own business fixed up, gentlemen; but I'll go by myself, or maybe with Petr Ivanovich here, privately, just for a walk, to inquire whether the transient strangers are suffering any annoyances. Hey, Svistunov!

SVISTUNOV: What, sir?

CHIEF OF POLICE: Go call the police captain right away—but no, I need you. Tell some one outside to go for him as quickly as possible, and then come back here. (*The* SERGEANT OF POLICE *runs out at full speed.*)

* The Freemasons were prohibited in Russia as a society dangerous to the government. Apparently the freethinking judge refers to a masonic book. (Adapted from Sykes.)

ARTEMY FILIPPOVICH: Let's go, let's go, Ammos Fedorovich! There may be some trouble, for a fact.

AMMOS FEDOROVICH: Aw, what are you afraid of? Put clean nightcaps on the patients, and cover up your tracks.

ARTEMY FILIPPOVICH: To hell with your nightcaps! I ordered oatmeal porridge served to the patients, but all the same the corridors stink so of cabbage that you have to hold your nose!

AMMOS FEDOROVICH: Well, I'm easy for my part. As a matter of fact, whoever 'll look into a district court? But if he does happen to glance at any paper, he'll lose all joy in life. Here I've been sitting on the judge's bench for fifteen years, and if I merely look at a report, all I can do is wave my hand! Solomon himself couldn't make out what's truth in it and what isn't.

(*The* JUDGE, *the* SUPERVISOR OF CHARITABLE INSTITUTIONS, *the* SUPERINTENDENT OF SCHOOLS, *and the* POSTMASTER *go out, and at the door encounter the returning* SERGEANT OF POLICE.)

SCENE IV

CHIEF OF POLICE, BOBCHINSKY, DOBCHINSKY, *and* SERGEANT OF POLICE

CHIEF OF POLICE: Well, is the cab waiting?

SERGEANT OF POLICE: Yes, sir.

CHIEF OF POLICE: Go down to the street . . . or no, stop! Go bring in . . . But where are the others?. Are you just alone? I certainly ordered Prokhorov to be here. Where's Prokhorov?

SERGEANT OF POLICE: Prokhorov is in a private house, but he can hardly be put on the job now.

CHIEF OF POLICE: Why not?

SERGEANT OF POLICE: Because they carried him in this morning dead drunk. They've soused him with two tubs of water, but so far he hasn't sobered up.

CHIEF OF POLICE (*clutching his head*): Oh, my God, my God! Hurry into the street; or no, run first to my room—d'you hear?—and bring me my sword and my new hat. Well, Petr Ivanovich, let's be going!

BOBCHINSKY: Me too, me too! Let me go, too, Anton Antonovich!

CHIEF OF POLICE: No, no, Petr Ivanovich, you simply can't! It's bad form, and there's not room enough in the cab.

BOBCHINSKY: Never mind, never mind; I'll manage; I'll run along behind on my own prongs. I'd just like to peep through a chink in the door to see how he behaves. . . .

CHIEF OF POLICE (*to the* POLICEMAN, *who hands him his sword*): Run right off and get the patrolmen, and have each of them take . . . How my sword has been scratched! That damned cheat of a merchant, Abdulin: he sees that the Chief of Police has nothing but an old sword, but he won't send me a new one. Oh, what a sly gang! As it is, I think those swindlers are getting complaints ready now to yank out from under their coat-tails. Have every patrolman grab a street—deuce take it—I mean a broom—and tell 'em to sweep the whole street that leads to the inn, and sweep it clean. . . . D'you hear? And look out, you; oh, I know you! You're mighty chummy with everybody, but you'll steal spoons and stick 'em in your leggings! Look out; I've got sharp ears! . . . What did you do to the merchant Chernyayev, ha? He gave you two yards of cloth for your uniform, but you swiped the whole bolt. Look out! You take tips too big for your rank! Now, get out!

SCENE V

The same and POLICE CAPTAIN

CHIEF OF POLICE: Ah, Stepan Ilyich! Say, for God's sake, where've you been hiding out? Whoever heard the like!

POLICE CAPTAIN: Why, I was right outside the gates.

CHIEF OF POLICE: Well, listen here, Stepan Ilyich! An official has come from Petersburg. What arrangements have you made out there?

POLICE CAPTAIN: Why, just as you ordered. I sent Police Sergeant Pugovitsyn with the patrolmen to clean the sidewalk.

CHIEF OF POLICE: But where's Derzhimorda?

POLICE CAPTAIN: Derzhimorda has gone off on the fire wagon.

CHIEF OF POLICE: And Prokhorov's drunk?

POLICE CAPTAIN: He is.

CHIEF OF POLICE: How did you happen to allow that?

POLICE CAPTAIN: Why, God knows. Yesterday there was a fight in the suburbs; he went out to restore order, and came back drunk.

CHIEF OF POLICE: Well, listen, here's your job: Police Sergeant Pugovitsyn . . . he's tall, so you can post him on the bridge for the sake of law and order. Then clear away the old fence next to the shoemaker's as quick as you can, and put up a straw waymark as if surveyors were doing some leveling. The more pulling-down there is, the more it shows activity on the part of the governor of the town. Oh, my God! I had forgotten that there's about forty cartloads of every sort of rubbish heaped up against that fence! What a rotten town! You no sooner set up a monument of some kind, or simply a fence, than people bring on all manner of rubbish, the devil knows where from! (*He sighs.*) And if that traveling official asks the people in service whether they're satisfied, have 'em say, "We're satisfied with everything, your Honor." And if any one is not satisfied, I'll give him something afterwards to be dissatisfied about! . . . Ow, ow, ow, I'm a sinner, a sinner in many ways! (*He picks up the cardboard hatbox instead of his hat.*) Just grant, O Lord, that I may get all this off my hands as quickly as possible, and I'll set up such a candle as was never lighted before: I'll make every brute of a merchant contribute a hundred pounds of wax. Oh, my God, my God! Let's go, Petr Ivanovich! (*He attempts to put on the box instead of his hat.*)

POLICE CAPTAIN: Anton Antonovich, that's the box, not your hat.

CHIEF OF POLICE (*throwing away the box*): Box, is it? Oh, to hell with it! And if they ask why the church for the almshouse hasn't been built, for which an appropriation was made five years ago, don't forget to say that it was started, but it burned down. I even presented a report on the matter. Even so I suppose some idiot out of sheer stupidity will forget and say that it wasn't ever started. Yes, and tell Derzhimorda not to be too free with his fists; he's always making people see stars in the name of law and order, innocent and guilty alike. Let's go, let's go, Petr Ivanovich! (*He goes out, but returns.*) And don't let the soldiers out on the street without a stitch on; that dirty garrison will put on their uniforms just over their shirts, but with absolutely nothing below! . . . (*They all go out.*)

SCENE VI

ANNA ANDREYEVNA *and* MARYA ANTONOVNA, *who come in running*

ANNA ANDREYEVNA: Where are they? Where are they? Oh, my heavens! . . . (*Opening the door.*) Husband! Antosha, Anton! (*To her daughter, speaking quickly.*) It's your fault, it's all along of you! You would be rummaging for a pin or a neckerchief. (*She runs to the window and calls out.*) Anton, where are you going? Who's come? A government inspector? With a mustache! What sort of mustache?

Voice of the CHIEF OF POLICE: I'll tell you later, dearie.

ANNA ANDREYEVNA: Later? What d'you know about that! Later! I don't want to wait till later. . . . Tell me in a word; what is he, a colonel? Ha? (*With indifference.*) He's gone! I'll remember that against you! And this girl keeps saying, "Mamma dear, mamma, wait a minute, I'm pinning my neckerchief behind; I'll come right away." Here's your right away for you! And so we haven't found out a thing! Always your darned primping! You heard that the postmaster was here, and you had to go and prink before the mirror, twisting this way and that! She imagines that he's courting her; but he's making faces at you as soon as you turn your back.

MARYA ANTONOVNA: Well, what's to be done, mamma? It's all the same! We'll find out everything in two hours.

ANNA ANDREYEVNA: In two hours! I most humbly thank you! There's an obliging answer! I wonder you never thought of saying that we'd know better yet in a month! (*Leaning out of the window.*) Hey, Avdotya! Ha? What? Avdotya, haven't you heard that somebody has arrived? . . . You haven't? What a blockhead! He waved you off? Well, let him, you might have pumped him all the same. You couldn't find that out! Your head's full of nonsense—nothing but your beaux. Ha? They went away in a hurry? Well, you could have run after the cab. Now get along with you this minute! Listen: run and ask where they've gone; and find out everything; who the newcomer is and what he's like, d'you hear? Peek through a crack and find out everything: and what kind of eyes he has, black or not; and come back this minute, d'you hear? Hurry up, hurry up, hurry up, hurry up! (*She keeps shouting until the curtain falls, both of them still standing at the window.*)

ACT II

A small room at the inn. A bed, a table, a trunk, an empty bottle, top-boots, a clothes-brush, and other objects

SCENE I

OSIP (*lying on his master's bed*): Devil take me; I'm so hungry that there's a continual rumbling in my stomach as though the whole regiment were beginning to blow their trumpets. I s'pose we'll never get home, and that's all there is to it. What do you want me to do? You came here two months ago, all the way from Petersburg! You squandered your dough on the road, my boy, and now you sit with your tail between your legs and keep cool. There would have been plenty of money for fares; but no, you had to spread yourself in every town! (*Taking him off.*) "Hey, Osip, run along and look up the best room for me, and order the best dinner possible. I can't eat a poor dinner; I have to have the best." That would be all right if he were really something decent, but he's just a junior clerk. You get acquainted with some traveler or other—then out with the cards, and first you know you're cleaned out! Bah! I'm sick of such a life! To be sure, it's better in the country: although there's not much society, there's less anxiety; you get yourself a woman and spend your life lying on the sleeping-shelf of the stove and eating meat pies. Of course if anybody wanted to argue about it and get at the truth, living in Petersburg is the best of all. If one only had money, life would be very fine and polished: there are theatres, with dancing dogs, and everything you like. All conversation's smart 'n elegant, second only to that of the nobility. You walk into the Shchukin Bazaar, and the clerks shout "Honorable sir!" at you. Crossing on the ferry boat you sit down with an official. If you want company, walk into a shop: there a military man will tell you about the camp, and explain just what each star means, so that you can see it all as plain as your hand before your face. An old officer's wife will stroll in; and such a pretty housemaid may peep in. . . . Tra, la, la! (*He bursts out laughing and shakes his head.*) Very gallant manners, deuce take it! You never hear an impolite word; every one addresses you as an equal. If you get tired of walking, you take a cab and sit back like a gentleman; and if you don't want to pay the cabby, never mind: every house has front and rear gates, and you can slip through so fast no devil can follow you up. Only one thing is bad: you eat swell one day, but the next you may croak with hunger, like now, for instance. But he's always to blame. What's to be done with him? His dad will send him money, but instead of hanging on to it—nothing of the kind; off he goes on a spree. He rides in cabs, gets a theatre ticket every day, and then at the end of a week he sends me to the old-clothes shop to sell his new dress-coat. Sometimes he'll sell even his last shirt so that he's nothing to put on but his frock-coat and his overcoat. . . . That's the truth, by God! And such fine English cloth, too! One coat cost him one hundred and fifty rubles, but the old clo' dealer got it from him for twenty. As for the trousers, there's nothing to be said: they go for nothing. And why? Because he won't attend to business. Instead of going to his work, he strolls up and down the Nevsky Prospect and plays cards. If the old gentleman should find out—wow! He wouldn't consider the fact that you're an official, but he'd snatch up your little shirt-tail and give you such a hiding that you'd rub yourself for four days. If you're in the service, do your work. Here's the innkeeper now who says he won't give us anything more to eat until we pay for what we've had; but what if we don't pay? (*Sighing.*) Oh Lord, my God, if only I had some cabbage soup, good or bad! I think I could gobble up the world. There's a knock; that's him coming, sure. (*He hops off the bed in a hurry.*)

SCENE II

OSIP *and* HLESTAKOV

HLESTAKOV: Here, take this. (*He gives* OSIP *his hat and cane.*) So you've been lolling on the bed again?

OSIP: Why should I? Haven't I ever seen a bed before?

HLESTAKOV: You're lying, you were lolling! You see, it's all mussed up.

OSIP: What should I muss it for? Don't you suppose I know what a bed is? I have legs; I know how to stand up. What's your bed to me?

HLESTAKOV (*walking about the room*): See if there's any tobacco in the bag yonder.

OSIP: How could there be any? You smoked up the last four days ago.

HLESTAKOV (*walks about and purses up his lips in a variety of ways, finally speaking in a loud and determined voice*): Listen! . . . Hey, Osip!

OSIP: What do you want?

HLESTAKOV (*in a loud, but not so determined voice*): You go down there.

OSIP: Where?

HLESTAKOV (*in a voice quite lacking in determination, softer, and almost entreating*): Downstairs, to the bar . . . and tell them to . . . to send me my dinner.

OSIP: Oh no, I don't want to.

HLESTAKOV: How dare you, blockhead!

OSIP: Why, because it'll be all the same; even if I go, we won't get anything. The boss said he wouldn't give us any more dinners.

HLESTAKOV: How does he dare not give us any? That's nonsense.

OSIP: "I'm going to the Chief of Police," says he; "the gentleman hasn't paid anything for three weeks. You and your master are swindlers," he says, "and your master's a rascal. We've seen spongers and scoundrels like you before."

HLESTAKOV: And I'll bet you're happy, you brute, to be telling me all that now.

OSIP: He says: "A fellow like that will come, live high, run up a bill, and afterwards there's no driving him out. I'm not going to joke," he says; "I'm going to complain straight off and have him taken to the police station and then to jail."

HLESTAKOV: Well, that's enough. you blockhead! Get along with you and tell him! What a vulgar animal!

OSIP: It would be better for me to call the proprietor up here to you.
HLESTAKOV: Why call the proprietor? Go yourself and tell him.
OSIP: But really, sir . . .
HLESTAKOV: Well then, deuce take you, call the proprietor!
(OSIP *goes out.*)

SCENE III

HLESTAKOV *alone*

HLESTAKOV: It's awful how hungry I am! I thought that if I'd just take a walk my appetite would go; but no, damned if it would! If I hadn't gone on a spree at Penza, I'd have had the money to get home. That infantry captain hooked me for fair: he plays wonderful faro, the cheat! We sat down for a quarter of an hour in all, and he fleeced me clean. All the same I was crazy to have another go at him, but I didn't have the opportunity. What a rotten hick town! In their lousy shops they won't sell a thing on credit. I call that simply mean. (*He begins to whistle an air from "Robert the Devil," then "The Red Sarafan," and finally no particular tune.*) Nobody'll come.

SCENE IV

HLESTAKOV, OSIP, *and an* INN SERVANT

SERVANT: The proprietor told me to ask for your orders.
HLESTAKOV: Good day, my boy! How's your health?
SERVANT: Good, thank God.
HLESTAKOV: Well, how are things with the inn: everything going all right?
SERVANT: Yes, thank God, everything's all right.
HLESTAKOV: Many travelers?
SERVANT: Yes, enough.
HLESTAKOV: Listen, my boy, they haven't brought me my dinner yet, so please hurry up and bring it as quickly as possible; you see, I have something to attend to directly after dinner.
SERVANT: But the boss said he wasn't going to send up anything more. He came near going to the Chief of Police to-day with a complaint.
HLESTAKOV: But why complain? Just consider, my boy, what's the use? You see, I've got to eat. Otherwise I might get thin. I'm awfully hungry; and I'm not joking either.
SERVANT: Exactly, sir. But he said, "I shan't give him anything to eat until he's paid for what he's had." That's what his answer was.

HLESTAKOV: Well, you reason with him; talk him over.

SERVANT: What in the world shall I say to him?

HLESTAKOV: You put it to him seriously that I need to eat. The money is another matter. . . . He thinks that if a peasant like him can go without eating for a day, other people can. What an idea!

SERVANT: All right, I'll tell him.

SCENE V

HLESTAKOV *alone*

HLESTAKOV: It's rotten, all the same, if he won't give me anything at all to eat. I never was so hungry in my life. I wonder whether I could raise something on my clothes? Could I sell my trousers? No, I'd rather go hungry than not go home in my Petersburg suit. It's a pity that Joachim * wouldn't rent me a carriage. It would have been fine, confound it all, to drive up like a swell to some neighboring landowner's front door, with lanterns, and Osip behind in livery. I can imagine how excited they'd all get! "Who's there? What does he want?" And the footman would go in (*drawing himself up straight like a footman*) and announce: "Ivan Alexandrovich Hlestakov, from Petersburg; will you receive him?" They, country bumpkins as they are, don't even know what "will you receive him?" means. When any goose of a landowner goes to see them, he wallows straight into the parlor like a bear. I'd go up to some good-looking young daughter and say, "Madam, how happy I . . ." (*He rubs his hands and scrapes with one foot.*) Fah! (*Spitting.*) I'm sick at my stomach, I'm so hungry.

SCENE VI

HLESTAKOV, OSIP, *then the* SERVANT

HLESTAKOV: Well, what now?

OSIP: They're bringing dinner.

HLESTAKOV (*clapping his hands and making a slight jump in his chair*): Hurrah, they're bringing dinner!

SERVANT (*with plates and a napkin*): This is the last dinner the proprietor will send.

HLESTAKOV: Oh, the proprietor, the proprietor! . . . I spit on your proprietor! What have you got there?

SERVANT: Soup and roast.

HLESTAKOV: What, only two courses?

* "A celebrated horse and carriage dealer of St. Petersburg."—Sykes.

SERVANT: That's all, sir.

HLESTAKOV: What trash is this? I won't accept it. You tell him that this is the limit! . . . That's not enough.

SERVANT: No, the boss says that it's a lot.

HLESTAKOV: But why isn't there any sauce?

SERVANT: There isn't any sauce.

HLESTAKOV: Why isn't there any? I saw them preparing a lot of it myself when I passed by the kitchen. And in the dining-room this morning there were two rather short fellows eating salmon and a lot of other things.

SERVANT: Well, there is some, of course, and there isn't.

HLESTAKOV: What d'you mean, isn't?

SERVANT: There just ain't.

HLESTAKOV: And salmon, and fish, and cutlets?

SERVANT: They're for better people, sir.

HLESTAKOV: Oh, you blockhead!

SERVANT: Yes, sir.

HLESTAKOV: You contemptible little swine! Why do they eat when I don't? Why, damn it all, can't I do as they do? Aren't they travelers just like me?

SERVANT: Why, everybody knows that they ain't.

HLESTAKOV: What are they, then?

SERVANT: The regular sort! Everybody knows: they pay their bills!

HLESTAKOV: I don't care to argue with you, you blockhead. (*He helps himself to soup and begins to eat.*) What kind of soup is this? You've just poured water into the tureen: it hasn't any taste; it merely stinks. I don't want this soup; bring me some other.

SERVANT: I'll remove it, sir. The proprietor said, "If he doesn't want it, he needn't have it."

HLESTAKOV (*protecting the food with his hands*): Well, well, well . . . leave it, you blockhead! You may be used to treating other people like that; but I'm not that sort, my boy. . . . I advise you not to act like that with me. . . . (*He eats.*) My God, what soup! (*He continues eating.*) I think no man on earth to date has ever eaten such soup: there's some kind of feathers swimming around in it instead of grease! (*He cuts the chicken in the soup.*) Ow, ow, ow, what a bird! Give me the roast! There, Osip, there's a little soup left; take it yourself. (*He carves the roast.*) What kind of roast is this? This is no roast.

SERVANT: Why, what is it?

HLESTAKOV: The devil knows *what* it is, but it's not roast. It's roasted ax instead of ox. (*He eats.*) Swindlers, riffraff! What stuff they hand you! Your jaws begin to ache if you swallow a single bite.

(*He picks his teeth with his finger.*) Rascals! It's just like bark—you can't pull it out anyhow; and your teeth will turn black after such dishes. Swindlers! (*Wiping his mouth with his napkin.*) Isn't there anything more?

SERVANT: No.

HLESTAKOV: Riffraff! Rascals! And not even a little sauce or a pudding. Grafters! They simply fleece travelers.

(*The* SERVANT *and* OSIP *collect the dishes and carry them away.*)

SCENE VII

HLESTAKOV, *later* OSIP

HLESTAKOV: Really, I feel as if I hadn't eaten a thing: I've just whetted my appetite. If I had any small change, I'd send to the market for a bun.

OSIP (*coming in*): The Chief of Police has come on some errand; he's making inquiries and asking about you.

HLESTAKOV (*frightened*): Well, I declare! Has that brute of an innkeeper managed to complain already? What if he really drags me to jail! What then? I suppose, if he did it in a gentlemanly manner, I might . . . But no, no, I won't! There in town officers and people are strolling about, and I purposely played the swell and exchanged winks with a tradesman's daughter. . . . No, I won't. . . . But how in the world did he dare? What does he take me for, anyhow, a merchant or an artisan? (*He adopts a bold manner and straightens up.*) I'll go right to him and say, "How dare you? How dare . . . ?"

(*The door-handle turns;* HLESTAKOV *turns pale and shrinks.*)

SCENE VIII

HLESTAKOV, CHIEF OF POLICE, *and* DOBCHINSKY

Upon entering the room, the CHIEF OF POLICE *stands still. He and* HLESTAKOV *stare at each other wide-eyed in fright for several moments.*

CHIEF OF POLICE (*recovering somewhat and standing at attention*): Please accept my greetings!

HLESTAKOV (*bowing*): And mine to you, sir.

CHIEF OF POLICE: Pardon me. . . .

HLESTAKOV: Oh, certainly. . . .

CHIEF OF POLICE: It is my duty as the chief official of the town to see that travelers and members of the nobility experience no inconvenience. . . .

HLESTAKOV (*at first stammering a little, but finally speaking loudly*): But what's to be done? . . . It's not my fault. . . . I'll pay, honest. . . . They'll send me some money from the country. (BOBCHINSKY *peeks in at the door.*) He's more to blame: he sends me beef as tough as a wooden beam; as for soup, the devil knows what he slops into it; I should have thrown it out the window. He starves me out for days at a time. . . . And such queer tea: it smells of fish, but not of tea. Why should I? . . . What an idea!

CHIEF OF POLICE (*losing courage*): Pardon me, I'm really not to blame. There's always good beef in our market. Dealers from Holmogory* supply it, sober men and well-behaved. I don't know where he could get such as you describe. But if anything is not just right . . . Permit me to propose that I remove you to other lodgings.

HLESTAKOV: No, I won't. I know what you mean by other lodgings—the jail. But what right have you? How dare you? . . . Look here, I . . . I'm in the government service in Petersburg. (*Growing bolder.*) I, I, I . . .

CHIEF OF POLICE (*aside*): Oh, Lord my God, how angry he is! He's found out everything, those damned merchants have told him!

HLESTAKOV (*more bravely*): Even if you came with a whole regiment, I wouldn't go. I'll go straight to the Minister! (*Striking the table with his fist.*) What's the matter with you, anyway?

CHIEF OF POLICE (*drawing himself up straight and trembling in every limb*): Have mercy; don't ruin me! Consider my wife, my little children! . . . Don't make a man wretched!

HLESTAKOV: No, I won't go. The idea! What's all that to me? Because you have a wife and children, I have to go to jail—that's grand! (BOBCHINSKY *peeks through the door, then hides in fright.*) No, I humbly thank you, I won't go!

CHIEF OF POLICE (*trembling*): It's my inexperience, God knows, just my inexperience. The insufficiency of my income . . . Please, sir, judge for yourself: my official salary doesn't even buy our tea and sugar. If I've taken a few bribes, they were mere trifles, something or other for the table or for a suit of clothes. And as for the sergeant's widow who keeps a shop, whom I'm supposed to have flogged, that's all slander, God knows it is. All that was thought up by my enemies; they're people who are ready to make an attempt on my life.

HLESTAKOV: What of it? I have nothing to do with them. . . . (*Meditating.*) Still, I don't know why you're talking about your enemies and some sergeant's widow or other. A sergeant's widow is quite another matter, but you won't dare to flog me; you're a long way

* A small town in the province of Archangel, noted for its cattle. (Adapted from Sykes.)

from that job! . . . The idea! What a chap you are! . . . I'll pay, I'll pay the money, but I haven't it now. I'm sticking around here because I haven't a kopek.

CHIEF OF POLICE (*aside*): Oh, a sly trick! What a hint! He makes things hazy, and you can take 'em as you please! There's no knowing how to get at him. Well, I'll make a stab at it, no matter what happens. What will be, will be. I'll take a shot at random. (*Aloud.*) If you're really needing money or something else, I'm ready to help you this very minute. It's my duty to assist travelers.

HLESTAKOV: Lend me, do lend me some! I'll settle with the dirty innkeeper at once. I owe him only about two hundred rubles, a little more or less.

CHIEF OF POLICE (*producing some notes*): Exactly two hundred rubles, but don't trouble to count them.

HLESTAKOV (*taking the money*): I thank you heartily. I'll return the amount at once from the country. . . . This was a sudden embarrassment. . . . I see that you are a gentleman. Now things are very different.

CHIEF OF POLICE (*aside*): Well, thank God, he took the money! Now I think everything will go smoothly. I slipped him four hundred instead of two.

HLESTAKOV: Hey, Osip! (OSIP *comes in.*) Call that waiter here! (*To the* CHIEF OF POLICE *and* DOBCHINSKY.) But why are you standing? Do me the favor to be seated! (*To* DOBCHINSKY.) Do please sit down.

CHIEF OF POLICE: Oh, no, we're all right standing.

HLESTAKOV: Do please be seated. Now I see perfectly your candor and cordiality; I admit that at first I thought you had come to . . . (*To* DOBCHINSKY.) Sit down! (*The* CHIEF OF POLICE *and* DOBCHINSKY *sit down.* BOBCHINSKY *peeps through the door and listens.*)

CHIEF OF POLICE (*aside*): I'll have to be more daring. He wants us to consider him as traveling incognito. Very good, we can fake, too; we'll pretend we haven't the least idea who he is. (*Aloud.*) While strolling about on my official duties with Petr Ivanovich Dobchinsky, here, a landed proprietor of the vicinity, I came into the inn on purpose to inquire whether the travelers were being well entertained; because I'm not like some police chiefs who don't care about anything. Aside from my duty, out of a Christian love of humanity, I want every mortal to be given a good reception; and here, as if to reward me, chance has afforded me this pleasant acquaintance.

HLESTAKOV: I also am very glad. I confess that except for you, I should have had to stay here a long time: and I absolutely didn't know how I could pay.

CHIEF OF POLICE (*aside*): Why, how you talk! He didn't know how he was going to pay! (*Aloud.*) And may I venture to inquire where you are going?

HLESTAKOV: I'm going to my own village in the province of Saratov.

CHIEF OF POLICE (*aside, with an ironical expression of countenance*): To Saratov, he? And he doesn't blush! Oh, one needs a sharp ear with him! (*Aloud.*) You have undertaken a good task. Concerning the road, they say that while, on the one hand, there is unpleasantness because of the delay for horses, on the other, it's a distraction for the mind. I suppose that you're traveling chiefly for your own pleasure?

HLESTAKOV: No, my father wants to see me. The old gentleman is angry because so far I've not been promoted in Petersburg. He thinks that you've only to go there and they'll stick the Vladimir ribbon in your buttonhole. No—I'd like to send *him* to bustle about in the office!

CHIEF OF POLICE (*aside*): Listen to the yarns he's spinning! He's even tangling up his old daddy! (*Aloud.*) And shall you be gone long?

HLESTAKOV: Indeed, I don't know. You see, my father is obstinate and silly, the old duffer, stubborn as a post. I shall say to him right out: "Whether you like it or not, I can't live away from Petersburg. And why, as a matter of fact, must I ruin my life among peasants? Nowadays a man's needs are quite different: my soul thirsts for enlightenment."

CHIEF OF POLICE (*aside*): How well he strings it together! He lies and lies and never trips himself. And he's such an insignificant little fellow, I think I could squash him with my finger nail. Well, just hold on! I'll make you blab yet. I'll make you talk some more. (*Aloud.*) Your remark is quite correct. What can you do in the wilderness? Now, take it here, for instance: you work all night long; you labor for your fatherland; you spare yourself in no way; but as for your reward, no one knows when you'll get it. (*He glances about the room.*) It strikes me this room is a little damp?

HLESTAKOV: A beastly room, and the bugs surpass any I've ever seen: they bite like bulldogs.

CHIEF OF POLICE: You don't say! Such a cultured guest, and he suffers, from what?—from worthless bugs that should never have been born into the world! Isn't it also a little dark in this room?

HLESTAKOV: Yes, quite dark. The proprietor has introduced the custom of not allowing candles. Sometimes when I want to do something, to read a little, or if I take a fancy to compose something, I can't: it's dark, always dark.

CHIEF OF POLICE: Might I ask you—? But no, I'm unworthy.
HLESTAKOV: Why, what is it?
CHIEF OF POLICE: No, no, I'm unworthy; I'm unworthy.
HLESTAKOV: But what in the world is it?
CHIEF OF POLICE: I might venture . . . At my house there's a room that would just suit you: light, and quiet. . . . But no, I realize that it would be too great an honor for me. . . . Don't be angry! Honest to God, I offered it only in the simplicity of my soul.
HLESTAKOV: On the contrary, I'll accept with pleasure, if you please. It would be much more agreeable for me in a private home than in this dump.
CHIEF OF POLICE: How glad I shall be! And how glad my wife will be, too! That's my disposition, hospitable from my childhood, especially if the guest is a man of culture. Don't think I'm saying this in flattery: no, I haven't that vice; I am expressing myself out of the fullness of my heart.
HLESTAKOV: I thank you heartily. I'm the same: I don't like two-faced people. I'm delighted with your candor and cordiality; and I confess I ask nothing more than to be shown devotion and respect, respect and devotion.

SCENE IX

The same and the INN SERVANT, *introduced by* OSIP

BOBCHINSKY *continues peeking through the door.*

SERVANT: Did you send for me, sir?
HLESTAKOV: Yes; bring me my bill.
SERVANT: I handed it to you long ago for the second time.
HLESTAKOV: I don't remember your stupid bills. Tell me: how much is it?
SERVANT: On the first day you ordered dinner; on the second you just ate a little kippered salmon; and then you began to order everything on credit.
HLESTAKOV: Blockhead! He's begun to reckon it all over again. What does it come to in all?
CHIEF OF POLICE: Don't trouble yourself; he can wait. (*To the* SERVANT.) Go away; the money'll be sent down.
HLESTAKOV: Yes, indeed; just so. (*He puts away the money. The* SERVANT *goes out;* BOBCHINSKY *peeks through the door.*)

SCENE X

CHIEF OF POLICE, HLESTAKOV, DOBCHINSKY

CHIEF OF POLICE: Now wouldn't you like to inspect some of the institutions in our town, the charitable ones and others?

HLESTAKOV: What is there to see?

CHIEF OF POLICE: So you can see how things go with us . . . what sort of order . . .

HLESTAKOV: With great pleasure; I'm ready.

(BOBCHINSKY *sticks his head through the door.*)

CHIEF OF POLICE: Also, if you wish it, we can go next to the district school to see how the sciences are taught there.

HLESTAKOV: Yes, let's do so.

CHIEF OF POLICE: Then, if you want to visit the prison and the city jails, you will see how we treat criminals.

HLESTAKOV: But why the city jails? We'd better inspect the charitable institutions.

CHIEF OF POLICE: Just as you please. How do you intend to go: in your own carriage, or with me in a cab?

HLESTAKOV: Well, I think I'd better go with you in a cab.

CHIEF OF POLICE (*to* DOBCHINSKY): Well, Petr Ivanovich, there'll be no place for you.

DOBCHINSKY: Never mind; I'm all right.

CHIEF OF POLICE (*softly to* DOBCHINSKY): Listen: you run lickety-split and carry two notes, one to Zemlyanika at the hospital and the other to my wife. (*To* HLESTAKOV.) May I venture to ask your permission to write in your presence a line to my wife, bidding her prepare for the reception of an honored guest?

HLESTAKOV: Certainly. . . . Here's the ink; but as for paper, I don't know . . . How about the back of this bill?

CHIEF OF POLICE: I'll write on that. (*He writes, meanwhile talking to himself.*) Now we'll see how things will go after lunch and a big-bellied bottle! We have some provincial Madeira—not much to look at, but it'll knock an elephant off its feet. If I could only find out what sort of fellow he is, and how much I need to be afraid of him. (*Having written, he hands the notes to* DOBCHINSKY, *who approaches the door; but at that moment the door falls off its hinges, and* BOBCHINSKY, *who has been listening on the other side, flies into the room with it. All utter exclamations.* BOBCHINSKY *picks himself up.*)

HLESTAKOV: I hope you didn't hurt yourself anywhere?

BOBCHINSKY: Not at all, not at all, sir, not the least derangement, sir; only a little scratch over my nose. I'll run over to Christian Ivanovich; he has some kind of little plaster, sir, and it'll soon get well.

CHIEF OF POLICE (*to* HLESTAKOV, *after making a reproachful sign to* BOBCHINSKY): That's nothing, sir. If you please, we'll go now. And I'll tell your servant to bring your trunk over. (*To* OSIP.) My good fellow, just bring everything over to my house, to the Police Chief's residence—any one will show you the way. After you, sir. (*He permits* HLESTAKOV *to go out first and follows him; then, turning around, he speaks reproachfully to* BOBCHINSKY.) That's you all over! You couldn't find any other place to fall! And there you sprawled like the devil knows what! (*He goes out,* BOBCHINSKY *after him. The curtain falls.*)

ACT III

The same room as in Act I

SCENE I

ANNA ANDREYEVNA *and* MARYA ANTONOVNA *are standing at the window in the same positions.*

ANNA ANDREYEVNA: Well now, we've been waiting a whole hour, and all the time you with your silly primping: you were all dressed, but no! you still had to rummage! . . . I shouldn't have listened to her at all. What an annoyance! As if on purpose, there's not a soul about! It's as if everything had died.

MARYA ANTONOVNA: But really, mamma, in two minutes we'll find out everything. Avdotya must be back soon. (*She looks out of the window and exclaims.*) Oh, mamma, mamma! Some one's coming, there at the end of the street!

ANNA ANDREYEVNA: Where is he? You're always having crazy notions. Well, sure enough. But who is it? Medium-sized . . . in a dress coat. . . . Who can it be? Ha? Isn't that annoying! Who in the world can it be?

MARYA ANTONOVNA: It's Dobchinsky, mamma!

ANNA ANDREYEVNA: Dobchinsky, my foot! You're always imagining things! . . . It can't be Dobchinsky. (*She waves her handkerchief.*) Hey, you, come here! Hurry up!

MARYA ANTONOVNA: Really, mamma, it is Dobchinsky.

ANNA ANDREYEVNA: There you go, always quarreling! I tell you it's *not* Dobchinsky.

MARYA ANTONOVNA: Aha, mamma, what did I tell you? You see, it *is* Dobchinsky.

ANNA ANDREYEVNA: Well, yes, it's Dobchinsky; I see now—why are you arguing about it? (*Shouting out of the window.*) Hurry up, hurry up; you're too slow! Well, where are they? Huh? Go ahead and talk from where you are. What? Very severe? Huh? And my husband? Where's my husband? (*Leaning slightly out of the window, with vexation.*) What a boob: until he gets into the very room, he won't tell a thing!

SCENE II

The same and DOBCHINSKY

ANNA ANDREYEVNA: Now, please tell me: well, aren't you ashamed? I relied on you as a decent man. They all rode off in a hurry, and you after them; and I can't get a sensible word from anybody since. Aren't you ashamed? I christened your Johnny and your Lizzie, and then you act like that with me!

DOBCHINSKY: Heavens, godmother, I ran so fast to prove my respect for you that I can't catch my breath. My respects, Marya Antonovna.

MARYA ANTONOVNA: How do you do, Petr Ivanovich.

ANNA ANDREYEVNA: Well, what's the news? Tell me what happened and how.

DOBCHINSKY: Anton Antonovich has sent you a note.

ANNA ANDREYEVNA: But what's the man like? Is he a general?

DOBCHINSKY: No, he's not a general; but he's not inferior to one in education and elegant manners.

ANNA ANDREYEVNA: Aha! Then he must be the one they wrote to my husband about.

DOBCHINSKY: The very same. I was the first to discover the fact, along with Petr Ivanovich.

ANNA ANDREYEVNA: Well, tell us what happened and how.

DOBCHINSKY: Well, thank God, everything is all right. At first he wanted to treat Anton Antonovich rather rough; yes, he did. He got angry and said that everything was bad at the inn, that he wouldn't go to his house, and wouldn't go to jail on his account; but afterwards, when he found out Anton Antonovich's innocence, and had talked a little more to the point with him, he changed his attitude all at once, and, thank God, everything came out fine. Now they've gone to have a look at the charitable institutions. . . . I admit that Anton Antonovich was thinking that there had been some secret denunciation; I was a little bit scared myself.

ANNA ANDREYEVNA: What have you to be afraid of? You're not in the service.

DOBCHINSKY: Well, you know how it is when a bigwig talks: you feel scared.

ANNA ANDREYEVNA: Oh, the idea! . . . That's all nonsense. Now tell us: what's he like? Is he old or young?

DOBCHINSKY: Young—a young man, about twenty-three years old; but he talks just like an old man. "By all means," he says, "I'll go there, and there, too" . . . (*waving his hands*) and he says it all so grandly. "I like to write and to read," he says, "but I'm annoyed by the darkness of the room."

ANNA ANDREYEVNA: But what does he look like? Is he light or dark-complexioned?

DOBCHINSKY: No, more of a chestnut. And he has such quick eyes, like some little animal's; they're positively disconcerting.

ANNA ANDREYEVNA: Well, what's he written me in this note? (*She reads.*) "I hasten to inform you, my dear, that my situation was altogether lamentable; but trusting in God's clemency, item, for two salted cucumbers and for half a portion of caviar, twenty-five kopeks—" (*Pausing.*) I don't understand a thing: what's this about pickles and caviar?

DOBCHINSKY: Oh, Anton Antonovich just wrote that on a piece of scratch paper to save time: some sort of bill had been written on it.

ANNA ANDREYEVNA: Oh, I see. (*Continuing her reading.*) "But trusting in God's clemency, it looks as if everything would come out all right. Hurry and get a room ready for an important guest, the one hung with yellow wall paper; you needn't go to any extra trouble for dinner because we're going to have a bite at the hospital, with Artemy Filippovich, but order a lot of wine; tell the dealer Abdulin to send his very best; if he doesn't, I'll overhaul his whole cellar. Kissing your little hand, sweetheart, I remain your Anton Skvoznik-Dmukhanovsky." . . . Oh, good heavens! We'll have to hurry! Hey, who's there? Mishka!

DOBCHINSKY (*running to the door and shouting*): Mishka! Mishka! Mishka!

(MISHKA *comes in.*)

ANNA ANDREYEVNA: Listen: run to the merchant Abdulin . . . wait, I'll give you a note. (*She sits down at the table and writes a note, talking meanwhile.*) Give this note to the coachman, Sidor, and have him run to the merchant Abdulin's and get some wine. You yourself go at once and get the room in fine shape for a guest. Put up a bed and a washstand, and so forth.

DOBCHINSKY: Well, Anna Andreyevna, I'll hurry off now to see how the inspection's going on.

ANNA ANDREYEVNA: Go along, go along! I'm not keeping you!

SCENE III

ANNA ANDREYEVNA *and* MARYA ANTONOVNA

ANNA ANDREYEVNA: Now, Mashenka, we'll have to see about the way we're dressed. He's a Petersburg dandy; God forbid he should laugh at anything! The most becoming thing you can put on is your blue dress with the little flounces.

MARYA ANTONOVNA: Fudge, mamma, the blue! I don't like it at all! Lyapkin-Tyapkin's daughter wears blue, and so does Zemlyanika's. No, I'd better put on my flowered dress.

ANNA ANDREYEVNA: The flowered dress! . . . Really, you're saying that to be spiteful. The other'll be much better, because I want to wear my straw-colored; I'm very fond of straw color.

MARYA ANTONOVNA: Oh, mamma, it doesn't become you at all!

ANNA ANDREYEVNA: It doesn't become me?

MARYA ANTONOVNA: No, it doesn't; I'll bet anything you please, it doesn't; you've got to have dark eyes to wear straw color.

ANNA ANDREYEVNA: Well, upon my word! And haven't I got dark eyes? As dark as can be. What nonsense she's talking! How can they be otherwise when I always tell my fortune by the queen of clubs?

MARYA ANTONOVNA: Why, mamma! You usually tell it by the queen of hearts!

ANNA ANDREYEVNA: Nonsense, absolute nonsense! I never was the queen of hearts! (*She hastily goes out with* MARYA ANTONOVNA *and continues talking in the wings.*) What's she imagining now! The queen of hearts! Heaven knows what she means! (*After they have gone out a door opens, and* MISHKA *is seen throwing out some trash. Through another door* OSIP *comes in with a trunk on his head.*)

SCENE IV

MISHKA *and* OSIP

OSIP: Which way?

MISHKA: This way, uncle, this way!

OSIP: Wait, let me get my breath first. Oh, what a dog's life! Every load seems heavy on an empty belly.

MISHKA: Well, uncle, what d'you say? Will the general be here soon?

OSIP: What general?

MISHKA: Why, your boss.

OSIP: My boss? Is he a general?

MISHKA: Well, isn't he?

OSIP: He is, only over the left.

MISHKA: Is that more or less than a real general?

OSIP: More.

MISHKA: You don't say! That's why they've kicked up such a rumpus.

OSIP: Listen, my boy; I see you're a smart fellow; just get me something to eat!

MISHKA: There's nothing ready for you yet, uncle. You aren't going to eat common chow, but when your boss sits down to the table, they'll give you the same as he gets.

OSIP: What kind of common food have you got?

MISHKA: Cabbage soup, porridge, and pies.

OSIP: Give us your cabbage soup, porridge, and pies! That's all right, I'll eat everything. Well, let's carry in the trunk. Is there another way out?

MISHKA: Yes. (*They carry the trunk into a room at one side.*)

SCENE V

The POLICEMEN *open both wings of the door.* HLESTAKOV *comes in, after him the* CHIEF OF POLICE, *the* SUPERVISOR OF CHARITABLE INSTITUTIONS, *the* SUPERINTENDENT OF SCHOOLS, DOBCHINSKY *and* BOBCHINSKY, *the latter with a plaster on his nose. The* CHIEF OF POLICE *shows the* POLICEMEN *a piece of paper on the floor; they run to pick it up, bumping each other at full speed.*

HLESTAKOV: Very good institutions. I'm delighted that you show visitors everything in the town. They didn't show me anything in the other towns.

CHIEF OF POLICE: In other towns, I venture to inform you, the city managers and the other officials are more concerned about their own profit; but here, I may say, there is no other thought but to deserve by good order and vigilance the attention of the authorities.

HLESTAKOV: The lunch was very good. I quite overate myself. Do you fare like that every day?

CHIEF OF POLICE: That was especially for our welcome guest.

HLESTAKOV: I'm fond of eating. That's what we live for: to cull the flowers of pleasure. What was that fish called?

ARTEMY FILIPPOVICH (*running up*): Aberdeen cod, sir.

HLESTAKOV: Very tasty. Where was it we had lunch—in the hospital?

ARTEMY FILIPPOVICH: Just so, sir, in the charity hospital.

HLESTAKOV: I remember, I remember, there were some beds there. Have the patients all recovered? It seems to me there weren't many.

ARTEMY FILIPPOVICH: About ten remain, no more; the rest have all got well. That's the way it's arranged: such order! From the time I undertook the management—incredible as it may seem to you—all of them have been getting well, like flies.* A patient can hardly enter the hospital before he's cured, not so much by the medicines as by the reliability of the management.

CHIEF OF POLICE: The obligations of a chief of police are, I venture to inform you, simply head-breaking! So many different things devolve on him, concerning sanitation alone, repairs, and reconstruction . . . in a word, the wisest man might find himself in a quandary; but, thanks be to God, everything is coming out splendidly. Any other police chief, of course, would look out for his own profit; but—would you believe it?—even when I lie down to sleep I think: "O Lord my God, how can I bring it to pass that the authorities may perceive my zeal and be satisfied?" . . . Whether they will reward me or not is, of course, up to them; but at least I shall be at peace in my own heart. When there is order everywhere in the city, the streets swept clean, the people under arrest well cared for, and few drunkards . . . why, what more can I do? And in truth, I want no honors. Of course, honors are alluring, but compared to virtue, they are all ashes and vanity.

ARTEMY FILIPPOVICH (*aside*): Oho, the grafter, how thick he spreads it! God gave him a gift for it!

HLESTAKOV: That is true. I admit that I myself like to philosophize once in a while: I toss things off sometimes in prose, sometimes in verse.

BOBCHINSKY (*to* DOBCHINSKY): Correct, all correct, Petr Ivanovich! Such remarks . . . one can see he's studied the sciences.

HLESTAKOV: Tell me, please, don't you ever have any amusements or social gatherings—where one might, for instance, play a game of cards?

CHIEF OF POLICE (*aside*): Aha, my boy, we know what windowpane you're pebbling now! (*Aloud.*) God forbid! There's not even a rumor about such social gatherings here! I've never had cards in my hands; I don't even know how to play cards. I never could even look at them calmly; and if I ever happen to catch sight of such a thing as a king of diamonds, such disgust comes over me that I simply have to spit. It happened once that to amuse the children I built a little house of cards, but afterwards I had the damnedest dreams all night long. Deuce take them! How can people kill such precious time with them?

LUKA LUKICH (*aside*): But you cleaned me out of a hundred rubles yesterday, you scoundrel!

* The humor lies in the reference to the usual Russian phrase, "They die like flies." (Adapted from Sykes.)

CHIEF OF POLICE: I could use that time better in the service of the state.

HLESTAKOV: However, you put it too strongly. . . . All depends upon the way in which you look at the thing. If, for instance, you pass when you ought to raise your ante . . . then, of course . . . No, I disagree: sometimes playing is very tempting.

SCENE VI

The same, ANNA ANDREYEVNA, *and* MARYA ANTONOVNA

CHIEF OF POLICE: I venture to present my family: my wife and daughter.

HLESTAKOV (*making a bow*): How fortunate I am, madam, to have, as it were, the pleasure of seeing you.

ANNA ANDREYEVNA: It is even more agreeable for us to see such a personage.

HLESTAKOV (*strutting*): Pardon me, madam, quite the contrary; my pleasure is greater.

ANNA ANDREYEVNA: How can that be, sir! You are pleased to say that out of compliment. Won't you please be seated?

HLESTAKOV: Merely to stand beside you is happiness: nevertheless, if such be unmistakably your wish, I shall be seated. How happy I am at last to be sitting beside you!

ANNA ANDREYEVNA: Really, sir, I cannot take that compliment to myself. . . . I suppose that after the capital, a tour of the country has seemed very unpleasant?

HLESTAKOV: Exceedingly unpleasant. Accustomed to live, *comprenez-vous,* in society and suddenly to find oneself on the road: dirty eating-houses, the darkness of ignorance . . . I confess, that were it not for this circumstance (*glancing at* ANNA ANDREYEVNA *and posing*) which has compensated me for everything . . .

ANNA ANDREYEVNA: Indeed, how unpleasant it must have been for you.

HLESTAKOV: However, madam, at this minute it is very pleasant for me.

ANNA ANDREYEVNA: Oh, really, sir! You do me too much honor. I do not deserve it.

HLESTAKOV: Why do you not deserve it? You do deserve it, madam.

ANNA ANDREYEVNA: I live in the country. . . .

HLESTAKOV: But the country also has its hillocks and its streamlets. . . . Of course, who'd compare it with Petersburg? Oh, Petersburg! What a life, truly! You may think that I am only a copying clerk;

but no, I'm on a friendly footing with the chief of my department. He'll clap me on the shoulder and say, "Come have dinner with me, my boy!" I drop in at the office for two minutes, only long enough to say how things are to be done. And there the copy-clerk, poor rat, goes scribbling away with his pen, tr, tr. . . . They even wanted to make me a collegiate assessor; * but I thought, what for? And the porter flies up the stairs after me with a brush: "If you please, Ivan Alexandrovich," he says, "I'll clean your boots." (*To the* CHIEF OF POLICE.) Why are you standing, gentlemen? Please be seated.

CHIEF OF POLICE, ARTEMY FILIPPOVICH, LUKA LUKICH (*speaking together*): Our rank is such that we can stand. We'll just stand. Please don't disturb yourself.

HLESTAKOV: All rank aside, I beg you to be seated. (*The* CHIEF OF POLICE *and all sit down.*) I don't like ceremony. On the contrary, I try and try to slip through unnoticed. But it's impossible to hide oneself, quite impossible! I can hardly go out anywhere but they begin saying, "There goes Ivan Alexandrovich!" Once they even took me for the commander-in-chief: the soldiers jumped out of the guard-rooms and presented arms. Afterwards an officer with whom I am well acquainted said to me: "Well, my boy, we positively took you for the commander-in-chief."

ANNA ANDREYEVNA: You don't say!

HLESTAKOV: I'm acquainted with the pretty actresses. You see, I've written a few theatrical sketches. . . . I often see literary people. I'm on friendly terms with Pushkin. I often say to him, "Well, now Pushkin, my boy, how goes it?" "Oh, so-so, old chap," he'll reply, "just so-so. . . ." He's a great character!

ANNA ANDREYEVNA: And so you even write? How delightful it must be to be an author! Do you really contribute to the magazines?

HLESTAKOV: Yes, I contribute to the magazines. Besides, my works are numerous: *The Marriage of Figaro, Robert the Devil, Norma.*† I don't even remember all their titles. And it was all by accident: I didn't want to write, but the theatre management said, "Please write something, old boy." So I thought to myself, "Well, go ahead, old fellow." And then all of a sudden, one evening, I think it was, I wrote the whole thing and astonished everybody. I have extraordinary ease in thinking. Everything that has appeared under the name of Baron Brambeus ‡—*The Frigate Hope,*§ and the *Moscow Telegraph* ¶ . . . I wrote all that.

* The eighth rank in the Russian service; Hlestakov is in the fourteenth!
† Operas by Mozart, Meyerbeer, and Bellini. (Adapted from Sykes.)
‡ Pseudonym of the popular author, Sienkowski (1800-1858).
§ A novel by Bestuzhev.
¶ A newspaper.

ANNA ANDREYEVNA: You don't say! And so you were Brambeus?

HLESTAKOV: Of course; I correct all their articles. Smirdin * pays me forty thousand for doing it.

ANNA ANDREYEVNA: I dare say *Yury Miloslavsky* † is your work also.

HLESTAKOV: Yes, that's my work.

ANNA ANDREYEVNA: I guessed it at once.

MARYA ANTONOVNA: But, mamma, it says on the binding that it was written by Mr. Zagoskin.

ANNA ANDREYEVNA: There you go: I knew that you'd argue even here.

HLESTAKOV: Oh, yes, that is true: that is Zagoskin's; but there's another *Yury Miloslavsky,* and that's mine.

ANNA ANDREYEVNA: Well, it's certain that I read yours. So well written!

HLESTAKOV: I confess that I exist by literature. Mine is the foremost house in Petersburg. It's even known as Ivan Alexandrovich's house. (*Turning to all present.*) Do me the favor, ladies and gentlemen, to come to see me when you are in Petersburg. I also give balls.

ANNA ANDREYEVNA: I suppose that balls there must be given with remarkable taste and magnificence?

HLESTAKOV: It's simply beyond description. On the table, for instance, is a watermelon—a watermelon costing seven hundred rubles. Soup ready in the tureen has come directly from Paris by steamer; raise the lid and there's a fragrant steam the like of which you can't find in nature. I go to balls every day. We've formed our own whist club: the Minister of Foreign Affairs, the French Ambassador, the English, the German Ambassadors, and I. We nearly kill ourselves playing; really, you never saw anything like it. As I run up the stairs to my fourth-story apartment, I just say to the cook: "Here, Mavrushka, my overcoat! . . ." What am I lying about! I quite forgot that I live on the second floor. My staircase alone is worth . . . But it would be curious to glance into my hall before I'm awake mornings: counts and princes jostle each other and hum there like bees, you can hear nothing but buzz, buzz. . . . Sometimes even the Minister . . . (*The* CHIEF OF POLICE *and others timidly rise from their chairs.*) My mail even comes addressed to "Your Excellency." Once I was even the director of a department. It's strange: the director went away—no one knows where. Well, naturally there was a lot of talk as to who should occupy the post. Many of the generals applied eagerly and got it, but when they started to work, it was no go—too hard. The job looks easy enough, but just examine it; why, it's the very deuce! After-

* A noted St. Petersburg publisher. † A famous historical novel.

wards they saw there was nothing to do but give it to me. And that very minute they sent messengers through the streets, messengers, messengers, and messengers . . . you can imagine for yourself: thirty-five thousand messengers! What a situation, I ask you! "Ivan Alexandrovich, go take charge of the department!" I confess that I felt somewhat uneasy. I came out in my dressing gown. I wanted to decline, but I thought, this will get to the tsar; and then, there's the service record! . . . "Very well, gentlemen, I accept the post," I said; "I accept it," I said; "So be it," I said; "I accept; only look out for me; I have sharp ears! You know me. . . ." And that's the way it was: it used to be, when I walked through the department, as if an earthquake had struck them: every one was trembling and shaking like a leaf. (*The* CHIEF OF POLICE *and the others shake with fear;* HLESTAKOV *grows more excited.*) Oh, I don't like to joke; I gave them all a bawling-out. The Council of State itself is afraid of me. And why not, indeed? Because I'm that kind of man. I don't care for anybody. . . . I tell 'em all, "I know my business; shut up!" I go everywhere, everywhere! I drive to the Palace every day. Why, to-morrow they're going to make me a field-mar— (*He slips and almost sprawls upon the floor, but the officials respectfully support him.*)

CHIEF OF POLICE (*approaching, trembling in every limb, and striving to speak out*): You—your—your . . .

HLESTAKOV (*in a rapid, abrupt tone*): What is it?

CHIEF OF POLICE: You—your—

HLESTAKOV (*in the same tone*): I can't make out anything; it's all nonsense.

CHIEF OF POLICE: You . . . your . . . your Excellency, don't you wish to rest? . . . Here's your room, and everything that you need.

HLESTAKOV: Rest—bosh! All right. I'm willing to have a rest. Your lunch, gentlemen, was good. . . . I'm satisfied, I'm satisfied. . . . (*Declaiming.*) Aberdeen! Aberdeen cod! (*He goes into a side room, followed by the* CHIEF OF POLICE.)

SCENE VII

The same without HLESTAKOV *and the* CHIEF OF POLICE

BOBCHINSKY (*to* DOBCHINSKY): There's a man for you, Petr Ivanovich! That's what I call a man! Never in my life have I been in the presence of so important a personage; I all but died of fright. What do you think his rank may be, Petr Ivanovich?

DOBCHINSKY: I think almost a general.

BOBCHINSKY: And I think a general isn't fit to pull off his boots;

but if he's a general, he's a generalissimo. Did you hear how he squashed the Council of State? Let's go quick and tell Ammos Fedorovich and Korobkin. Good-by, Anna Andreyevna!

DOBCHINSKY (*to* ANNA ANDREYEVNA): Good-by, godmother!

(*They both go out.*)

ARTEMY FILIPPOVICH (*to* LUKA LUKICH): It's simply terrifying, but just why, you can't tell, yourself. We haven't even got into our uniforms. Well, do you suppose he'll send off a report to Petersburg when he wakes up? (*They go out thoughtfully along with the* SUPERINTENDENT OF SCHOOLS, *saying as they go.*) Good-by, madam!

SCENE VIII

ANNA ANDREYEVNA *and* MARYA ANTONOVNA

ANNA ANDREYEVNA: Oh, what a charming man!

MARYA ANTONOVNA: Oh, what a darling!

ANNA ANDREYEVNA: But what refinement in everything he does! You can see at once he's a Petersburg swell. His manners, and all that. . . . Oh, how nice! I'm crazy over young men like him! I simply lose my head over them. And moreover, he took a fancy to me; I noticed that he kept glancing my way.

MARYA ANTONOVNA: Why, mamma, he was looking at me!

ANNA ANDREYEVNA: I'll thank you to be off with your nonsense. It's quite out of place here.

MARYA ANTONOVNA: No, mamma, really!

ANNA ANDREYEVNA: Well, I declare! God forbid we should quarrel about it! That will do! Why should he look at you? What reason would he have for looking at you?

MARYA ANTONOVNA: Really, mamma, he kept looking at me. First when he began to talk about literature, he gave me a look; and then when he was telling about how he played whist with the ambassadors, he looked at me again.

ANNA ANDREYEVNA: Well, maybe, once or twice, but that's all it amounted to. "Oh, I'll just take a look at her!" he said to himself.

SCENE IX

The same and the CHIEF OF POLICE

CHIEF OF POLICE (*coming in on tiptoes*): Sh, sh!

ANNA ANDREYEVNA: What is it?

CHIEF OF POLICE: I'm sorry I got him drunk. What if half he says is true? (*Reflecting.*) And why shouldn't it be true? When he's on a spree, a man brings everything to the surface: whatever is in his heart is on his tongue. Of course, he lied a little; but unless you lie a little bit, no conversation is possible. He plays cards with the Ministers and drives to the Palace. . . . And so really, the more you think about it . . . the devil knows who he is. . . . I don't know what's going on in my head; it's as if I were either standing on a sort of steeple or were just about to be hanged.

ANNA ANDREYEVNA: And I felt absolutely no timidity whatever; I simply saw in him an educated, high-toned man of the world, and his rank was nothing to me.

CHIEF OF POLICE: That's the way with you women! That word "women" sums it all up! They always fall for fiddle-faddle! They wise-crack about anything that comes into their noddles. They get off with a whipping, but the husband's as good as dead. You, sweet soul, behaved as familiarly with him as if he were another Dobchinsky.

ANNA ANDREYEVNA: I advise you not to be uneasy on that score. We know a thing or two. . . . (*Glancing at her daughter.*)

CHIEF OF POLICE (*to himself*): Well, what's the use of talking to you women! . . . Here's a fix, indeed! I haven't yet been able to get over my fright. (*He opens the door and speaks off stage.*) Mishka! Call Police Sergeants Svistunov and Derzhimorda: they're outside the gate somewhere or other. (*After a brief silence.*) Everything in the world has turned queer; you might expect a man to be something to look at; but such a lean, skinny fellow—how are you going to know who he is? If a man's military, the fact shows plainly enough; but when he puts on a dress coat, he's like a fly with his wings pulled off. He whooped it up such a long time at the inn a while ago, and faked up such a lot of fairy tales and bunk that you'd never make sense of it in a lifetime. But then he finally gave in. He even blabbed more than he needed to. Evidently he's a young man.

SCENE X

The same and OSIP

They all run to meet him, beckoning.

ANNA ANDREYEVNA: Come here, my good fellow.

CHIEF OF POLICE: Sh! . . . Well, what about it? Is he asleep?

OSIP: Not yet; he's stretching a bit.

ANNA ANDREYEVNA: Listen; what's your name?

OSIP: Osip, madam.

CHIEF OF POLICE (*to his wife and daughter*): That'll do for you! (*To* OSIP.) Well now, my boy, have they fed you well?

OSIP: They have, I thank you heartily; very well indeed.

ANNA ANDREYEVNA: Tell me: an awful lot of counts and princes call on your master, don't they?

OSIP (*aside*): What shall I say? If they've fed me well now, they'll do even better later. (*Aloud.*) Yes, even counts come.

MARYA ANTONOVNA: My dear Osip, how good-looking your master is!

ANNA ANDREYEVNA: And please tell us, Osip, how he . . .

CHIEF OF POLICE: Oh, please stop! You only mix me up with such silly talk. Now then, my friend! . . .

ANNA ANDREYEVNA: What rank has your master?

OSIP: Oh, he has the usual thing.

CHIEF OF POLICE: Oh, my God, you keep asking such silly questions! You won't let me get in a word to the point. Now, my friend, what sort of man is your master? . . . Strict? Does he like to bawl people out or doesn't he?

OSIP: Yes, he likes to have things orderly. He sees to it that everything around him is kept ship-shape.

CHIEF OF POLICE: I like your face very much. My friend, you must be a good fellow. Now, what—?

ANNA ANDREYEVNA: Listen, Osip, does your master wear his uniform at home?

CHIEF OF POLICE: Really, that'll do, chatterboxes that you are! This is a serious business: it's a question of a man's life. (*To* OSIP.) Well, now, my friend, I like you very much. When traveling there's no harm, you know, in taking an extra little glass of tea—the weather has turned cooler—so here's a couple of rubles for tea.

OSIP (*taking the money*): Thank you very much, sir! God grant you the best of health! I'm a poor man, and you've helped me.

CHIEF OF POLICE: Good, good, the pleasure is mine. Now what, my friend—?

ANNA ANDREYEVNA: Listen, Osip, what kind of eyes does your master like best?

MARYA ANTONOVNA: Osip, dear, what a darling little nose your master has!

CHIEF OF POLICE: Oh, stop! Let me! . . . (*To* OSIP.) Now please tell me, my boy: to what does your master pay the most attention, that is, what pleases him most in traveling?

OSIP: What he likes depends on circumstances. Most of all he likes to be well received; he likes good entertainment.

CHIEF OF POLICE: Good entertainment?

OSIP: Yes, sir. Now take me, for instance, I'm only a serf, but he sees that I'm well treated, too. Darned if he doesn't! Sometimes when we go to a place, he'll say: "Well, Osip, did they treat you well?" "Badly, your Honor!" "Hm," he'll say, "he's a bad host, Osip. Remind me of that when I get home." "Aha," I think to myself (*waving his hand*); "I should worry; I'm a plain man."

CHIEF OF POLICE: Very good, you're talking sense. There, I've given you something for tea; here's something more for biscuits.

OSIP: Why do you favor me, your Honor? (*He pockets the money.*) I'll drink your health.

ANNA ANDREYEVNA: Come to me, Osip, and I'll give you something, too.

MARYA ANTONOVNA: Osip, dear, take your master a kiss from me! (HLESTAKOV *is heard coughing in the next room.*)

CHIEF OF POLICE: Sh! . . . (*Rising upon tiptoe, and finishing the scene in a subdued voice.*) God forbid your making any noise! Go to your own rooms—you've said enough. . . .

ANNA ANDREYEVNA: Let's go, Mashenka! I told you that I noticed something in our guest that only we two can talk about.

CHIEF OF POLICE: Oh, they'll talk enough! I think if I went to listen to them, I'd have to stuff my ears. (*Turning to* OSIP.) Now, my friend. . . .

SCENE XI

The same, DERZHIMORDA *and* SVISTUNOV

CHIEF OF POLICE: Sh! You stamp with your boots like bow-legged bears! You make a thumping like dumping a ton of rocks out of a cart! Where the devil have you been?

DERZHIMORDA: I was acting on your orders. . . .

CHIEF OF POLICE: Sh! (*Putting his hand over the* POLICEMAN'S *mouth.*) You croak like a crow! (*Imitating him.*) "I was acting on your orders!" Roaring like an empty barrel! (*To* OSIP.) Now, my friend, run along and get everything ready for your master. Command everything there is in the house. (OSIP *goes out.*) As for you two, go stand on the doorstep and don't move! And don't let any outsider into the house, especially tradesmen! If you let in a single one, I'll . . . Only see to it that if any one comes with a complaint or even looks as if he had a complaint to present against me, throw him out on his neck! Sock it to him! Like that! (*Illustrating a kick.*) Do you get me? Sh . . . sh. . . . (*He goes out on tiptoe after the* POLICEMEN.)

ACT IV

The same room in the house of the CHIEF OF POLICE

SCENE I

Enter carefully, almost on tiptoe, AMMOS FEDOROVICH, ARTEMY FILIPPOVICH, *the* POSTMASTER, LUKA LUKICH, DOBCHINSKY, *and* BOBCHINSKY *in full dress uniforms. The whole scene proceeds in an undertone.*

AMMOS FEDOROVICH (*arranging them all in a semicircle*): For God's sake, gentlemen, make a circle as quickly as possible and put on your best manner! Confound him, he rides to the Palace and bawls out the Council of State! Draw up in military order; it must be in military order. You run over to that side, Petr Ivanovich; and you, Petr Ivanovich, stand right here.

(*Both* PETR IVANOVICHES *run on tiptoe.*)

ARTEMY FILIPPOVICH. If you're willing, Ammos Fedorovich, we ought to undertake something or other.

AMMOS FEDOROVICH: Just what exactly?

ARTEMY FILIPPOVICH: Everybody knows what.

AMMOS FEDOROVICH: Slip him something?

ARTEMY FILIPPOVICH: Well, yes, slip him something.

AMMOS FEDOROVICH: It's dangerous, deuce take it! He might raise Cain—a government man like him! But how about an offering on the part of the nobility for a memorial of some sort?

POSTMASTER: Or say this: "Here is some money left unclaimed at the post office."

ARTEMY FILIPPOVICH: Look out that he doesn't send *you* away somewhere by post! Listen: things aren't done like that in a well-regulated state. Why is there a whole squadron of us here? We should introduce ourselves one by one; and then, between man and man, everything is fixed, and nothing leaks out. That's the way it's done in a well-regulated society! Now you'll be the first to begin, Ammos Fedorovich.

AMMOS FEDOROVICH: It would be better for you: our august guest broke bread in your establishment.

ARTEMY FILIPPOVICH: It would be still better for you, Luka Lukich, as the enlightener of youth.

LUKA LUKICH: I can't, I can't, gentlemen! I confess I was so brought up that if I have to talk with a man one rank higher than mine, I get heart failure and my tongue seems to stick in the mud. No, gentlemen, you really must relieve me!

ARTEMY FILIPPOVICH: Yes, Ammos Fedorovich, there's no one but you. You have only to say a word, and Cicero fairly flies off your tongue!

AMMOS FEDOROVICH: What are you talking about! Cicero! See here, what have you thought up! What if I do get carried away sometimes, talking about my house dogs or my hunting hounds? . . .

ALL (*surrounding him*): No, not only about dogs; you can talk about the Tower of Babel, too. . . .* No, Ammos Fedorovich, don't abandon us, be a father to us! . . . No, Ammos Fedorovich!

AMMOS FEDOROVICH: Let me be, gentlemen!

(*At this moment steps and coughing are heard in* HLESTAKOV'S *room. All vie with each other in their haste to reach the door, crowding and trying to get out, which they do only with some squeezing. A few exclamations are heard in undertones.*)

Voice of BOBCHINSKY: Ow! Petr Ivanovich, you stepped on my foot, Petr Ivanovich!

Voice of ARTEMY FILIPPOVICH: Let me out, gentlemen; you've squeezed me as flat as a soul in Purgatory!

(*A few gasping exclamations of* "Ow! ow!" *are heard; finally all have been pushed out, and the room remains empty.*)

SCENE II

HLESTAKOV *alone, entering sleepy-eyed*

HLESTAKOV: I think I must have snored properly. Where did they get such mattresses and feather beds? I fairly perspired. They must have slipped me something strong at lunch yesterday; my head still goes bang. So far as I can see, a fellow can spend his time agreeably here. I like cordiality; and I admit I like it best of all when people gratify me out of sheer kind-heartedness rather than for their personal interest. The Chief of Police's daughter isn't half bad to look at, and even her mamma might perhaps . . . Well, I don't know, but I sure like this life.

SCENE III

HLESTAKOV *and the* JUDGE (AMMOS FEDOROVICH)

AMMOS FEDOROVICH (*upon entering, stops, and says to himself*): My God, my God! Make this come out right! My knees will hardly hold me up. (*Aloud, drawing himself up, and grasping his sword-hilt.*)

* "The allusion is to the Judge's skepticism."—Sykes.

I have the honor to introduce myself: Judge of the local District Court, Collegiate Assessor Lyapkin-Tyapkin.

HLESTAKOV: I beg you to sit down. So you're the Judge here?

AMMOS FEDOROVICH: In 1816 I was elected to a three-year term by the will of the nobility and I have held the post ever since.

HLESTAKOV: It's profitable to be Judge, isn't it?

AMMOS FEDOROVICH: After three terms I was presented with the order of Vladimir of the Fourth Class, with the commendation of the authorities. (*Aside.*) The money is in my fist, and my fist is on fire!

HLESTAKOV: I like the Vladimir. Now the Anna of the Third Class isn't so good.

AMMOS FEDOROVICH (*little by little thrusting forward his closed fist, aside*): O Lord God! I don't know where I'm sitting. It's as if I had live coals under me.

HLESTAKOV: What have you got in your hand?

AMMOS FEDOROVICH (*flustered, and letting some notes fall to the floor*): Nothing, sir.

HLESTAKOV: Nothing, you say? I see you've dropped some money.

AMMOS FEDOROVICH (*trembling all over*): Not at all, sir! (*Aside.*) O God, here I am in the dock, and they're bringing up the police cart to get me!

HLESTAKOV (*picking it up*): Yes, it's money.

AMMOS FEDOROVICH (*aside*): Well, it's all over! I'm lost and done for!

HLESTAKOV: I say, won't you lend it to me?

AMMOS FEDOROVICH (*hastily*): Certainly, why not, sir? . . . With the greatest pleasure. (*Aside.*) Now, bolder, bolder! Pull me through, Most Holy Mother!

HLESTAKOV: On the road, you know, I spent every kopek, on this and that. . . . Of course, I'll send it to you at once from my country home.

AMMOS FEDOROVICH: Please, sir, the idea! It's honor enough without repayment. . . . Of course, in my poor, weak way, by zeal and diligent service of the authorities . . . I shall always strive to deserve . . . (*He rises from his chair and draws himself up to an attitude of attention.*) I won't venture to disturb you longer by my presence. Have you no orders for me?

HLESTAKOV: What sort of orders?

AMMOS FEDOROVICH: I considered that you might have some orders for the local District Court.

HLESTAKOV: What for? I haven't any need of it at present; no, there's nothing. Thank you very much.

AMMOS FEDOROVICH (*bowing and going out, aside*): The town is ours!

HLESTAKOV (*when alone*): The Judge is a good fellow!

SCENE IV

HLESTAKOV *and the* POSTMASTER, *who, clad in his uniform, stands at attention, hand on sword*

POSTMASTER: I have the honor to introduce myself: Postmaster and Court Councilor Shpekin.

HLESTAKOV: Ah, do come in! I'm very fond of pleasant society. Be seated. I suppose you live here all the time?

POSTMASTER: Just so, sir.

HLESTAKOV: I like this little town. Of course, it's not very populous; but what of that? It's not the capital. It's not the capital, is it?

POSTMASTER: That's perfectly true.

HLESTAKOV: You find *bong tong* only in the capital, where there are no provincial geese. What's your opinion: isn't that right?

POSTMASTER: Quite right, sir. (*Aside.*) I see he's not a bit haughty: he asks about everything.

HLESTAKOV: You'll have to admit, I suppose, that it's possible to live happily even in a small town?

POSTMASTER: Just so, sir.

HLESTAKOV: In my opinion all one needs is to be respected and sincerely liked—isn't that right?

POSTMASTER: Absolutely right.

HLESTAKOV: I confess I'm glad that you're of my opinion. Of course they call me peculiar, but that's the kind of disposition I have. (*Looking into the* POSTMASTER'S *eyes and speaking to himself.*) Why not ask this postmaster for a loan? (*Aloud.*) A strange sort of thing has happened to me: I got entirely cleaned out on the road. Couldn't you lend me three hundred rubles?

POSTMASTER: Why, certainly; I'd consider it the greatest pleasure. Here you are, sir. I'm heart and soul at your service.

HLESTAKOV: I'm much obliged. I confess I hate like hell to deny myself anything when traveling; and why should I? How does that strike you?

POSTMASTER: Just so, sir.

(*He rises and stands at attention, hand on sword.*)

I won't venture to disturb you any longer by my presence. . . . Have you perchance some remarks to make upon the management of the post office?

HLESTAKOV: No, nothing.

(*The* POSTMASTER *bows and goes out.*)

HLESTAKOV (*lighting a cigar*): The Postmaster, it seems to me, is also a nice fellow; at any rate, he's obliging. I like such people.

SCENE V

HLESTAKOV *and* LUKA LUKICH, *who is almost pushed through the door. Behind him a voice says, half aloud,* "What are you afraid of?"

LUKA LUKICH (*drawing himself up in trepidation and holding tight to his sword*): I have the honor to introduce myself: Superintendent of Schools and Titular Councilor Hlopov.

HLESTAKOV: Oh, pleased to meet you. Sit down, sit down. Have a cigar? (*Handing him a cigar.*)

LUKA LUKICH (*undecidedly, to himself*): Well, I declare! I didn't expect this. Shall I take it or not?

HLESTAKOV: Go ahead, take it; that's a good cigar. Of course it's not like those you get in Petersburg. There, my dear man, I used to smoke little cigars at twenty-five rubles the hundred—they simply make you want to kiss your hand after smoking. Here's a candle; have a light! (*He holds out a candle to him.*)

(LUKA LUKICH *tries to light his cigar and trembles all over.*)

HLESTAKOV: But that's the wrong end!

LUKA LUKICH (*dropping the cigar in his fright, spitting, and waving his hand; aside*): Devil take everything! My damned timidity has ruined me!

HLESTAKOV: Well, I see you don't care for cigars. I confess they're my weakness. Also, where the fair sex is concerned, I simply can't be indifferent. How about you? Which do you like better, brunettes or blondes?

(LUKA LUKICH *finds himself in utter bewilderment as to what to say.*)

HLESTAKOV: No, tell me frankly which: brunettes or blondes?

LUKA LUKICH: I don't venture to judge.

HLESTAKOV: No, no, now, don't offer excuses! I wish positively to find out your taste.

LUKA LUKICH: I venture to inform you . . . (*Aside.*) Well, I myself don't know what I'm saying.

HLESTAKOV: Ah, ha! You don't want to say! I believe some little brunette has got you into a slight embarrassment. Admit it now: hasn't she?

(LUKA LUKICH *remains silent.*)

HLESTAKOV: Ah, ha! You blushed! You see! You see! Why don't you talk?

LUKA LUKICH: I got scared, your Hon— . . . Excel— . . . Gra— . . . (*Aside.*) My damned tongue has betrayed me!

HLESTAKOV: Got scared? Well, there is something in my eyes that inspires timidity. At least I know there's not a woman who can hold out against them, is there?

LUKA LUKICH: Quite right, sir.

HLESTAKOV: A very strange thing has happened to me: on the road I got cleaned out. Couldn't you lend me three hundred rubles?

LUKA LUKICH (*to himself, clutching at his pocket*): What a fix if I haven't got it! I have! I have! (*He produces and tremblingly hands over the notes.*)

HLESTAKOV: Thanks ever so much.

LUKA LUKICH (*drawing himself up, hand on sword*): I won't venture to disturb you longer by my presence.

HLESTAKOV: Good-by.

LUKA LUKICH (*hurries out almost running, speaking aside*): Well, thank God! Here's hoping he won't peep in on the classes!

SCENE VI

HLESTAKOV *and* ARTEMY FILIPPOVICH, *who draws himself up, hand on sword*

ARTEMY FILIPPOVICH: I have the honor to present myself: the Supervisor of Charitable Institutions, Court Councilor Zemlyanika.

HLESTAKOV: How do you do? Pray be seated.

ARTEMY FILIPPOVICH: I had the honor of escorting you, and of receiving you personally in the charitable institutions entrusted to my care.

HLESTAKOV: Ah, yes, I remember. You treated me to a very good lunch.

ARTEMY FILIPPOVICH: I'm happy to do my best in the service of my country.

HLESTAKOV: I like good cooking; I admit it's my weakness. . . . Tell me, please, weren't you a little shorter in height yesterday? It seems so to me.

ARTEMY FILIPPOVICH: It may well be. (*A brief silence.*) I may say that I spare nothing, and zealously fulfill my duties. (*He draws his chair nearer and speaks in a lower voice.*) The Postmaster here does absolutely nothing: all the business is greatly neglected: the mail is kept back—you can find it out for yourself. The Judge also, who was here before I came, does nothing but course hares; he keeps dogs in the court rooms, and his behavior, if I may admit it in your presence—of course, for the good of my country, I must do it, although he's both a relative and a friend of mine—his behavior is most reprehensible. There's a certain landowner here named Dobchinsky, whom you have seen; and no sooner does this Dobchinsky go out of his house somewhere, than the Judge goes over to sit with his wife, and I'm ready to swear . . . And you have only to look at the children: there's not one that looks like Dobchinsky, but every one of them, even the little girl, is the spit 'n image of the Judge.

HLESTAKOV: You don't say so! I never thought of it.

ARTEMY FILIPPOVICH: Then there's the Superintendent of Schools. . . . I don't know how the authorities could entrust him with such a responsibility: he's worse than a Jacobin, and he inspires in the youth such radical principles that it's hard even to express them. Don't you want me to put all this on paper for you?

HLESTAKOV: Yes, put it on paper. I'd be much pleased. You know, when I'm bored I like to read over something amusing. . . . What is your name? I've quite forgotten.

ARTEMY FILIPPOVICH: Zemlyanika.

HLESTAKOV: Ah, yes, Zemlyanika. And tell me, please, have you any children?

ARTEMY FILIPPOVICH: I should say so, sir! Five of them, two grown up.

HLESTAKOV: You don't say! Grown up! And what are they? . . . How do you . . .?

ARTEMY FILIPPOVICH: Do you wish to ask what their names are?

HLESTAKOV: Yes, what are their names?

ARTEMY FILIPPOVICH: Nikolay, Ivan, Elizaveta, Marya, and Perepetuya.

HLESTAKOV: That's nice.

ARTEMY FILIPPOVICH: I won't venture to disturb you any longer by my presence, depriving you of time dedicated to your sacred duties. . . . (*He bows and is about to go out.*)

HLESTAKOV (*accompanying him*): No, that's all right. That was all very funny, what you were telling me. Come and see me again. I enjoy it so much. (*He returns, and opening the door, calls after him.*) Hey, you! What's your name? I keep forgetting your name.

ARTEMY FILIPPOVICH: Artemy Filippovich.

HLESTAKOV: Do me a favor, Artemy Filippovich! A queer thing has happened to me: I got quite cleaned out on the road. Haven't you some money you could lend me—say four hundred rubles?

ARTEMY FILIPPOVICH: Yes.

HLESTAKOV: Well, how opportune! I thank you heartily.

SCENE VII

HLESTAKOV, BOBCHINSKY, *and* DOBCHINSKY

BOBCHINSKY: I have the honor to introduce myself: Petr Ivanovich Bobchinsky, a resident of this town.

DOBCHINSKY: Petr Ivanovich Dobchinsky, a landowner.

HLESTAKOV: Ah, yes, I've seen you before. I think you had a fall: well, how's your nose?

BOBCHINSKY: First rate! Don't feel any anxiety, please; it's quite well and dried up.

HLESTAKOV: I'm glad it's healed. I'm very glad. . . . (*Suddenly and abruptly.*) Have you any money on you?

DOBCHINSKY: What do you mean, money?

HLESTAKOV: Lend me a thousand rubles.

BOBCHINSKY: Good Lord, I haven't such a sum. But haven't you, Petr Ivanovich?

DOBCHINSKY: I haven't it about me, because my money, if you care to know, has been deposited with the Charitable Board.*

HLESTAKOV: Well, if you haven't a thousand, a hundred will do.

BOBCHINSKY (*rummaging in his pockets*): Haven't you a hundred rubles, Petr Ivanovich? I have only forty altogether, in notes.

DOBCHINSKY (*looking in his bill-fold*): Twenty-five rubles in all.

BOBCHINSKY: Just take a better look, Petr Ivanovich. I know there's a hole in your right-hand pocket, and really, something may have fallen through.

DOBCHINSKY: No, really, there's nothing in the hole.

HLESTAKOV: Well, it's all the same. I just asked. Good: sixty-five rubles will do. . . . That's all right. (*He takes the money.*)

DOBCHINSKY: I venture to ask your help about a very delicate matter.

HLESTAKOV: What is it?

DOBCHINSKY: It's a thing of very great delicacy, sir: my eldest son, you see, was born before my marriage. . . .

HLESTAKOV: Yes?

DOBCHINSKY: Of course, that's only so to speak, sir, because he was born absolutely the same as if in wedlock; and I afterwards fixed everything up properly by the lawful bonds of matrimony, sir. And so, you see, I now want him to be my son entirely, that is, legally, sir, and to bear my name, Dobchinsky, sir.

HLESTAKOV: Very good, let him; that's all right.

DOBCHINSKY: I shouldn't have troubled you, but I'm sorry for the boy, who has such talents. He fills us with the greatest hopes: he can

---

* This had charge of beggars, orphans, invalids, the insane.

repeat different poems by heart; and if he happens to get hold of a pocket knife, he makes a little cab right off, as skillfully as a juggler, sir. Petr Ivanovich here knows all about it.

BOBCHINSKY: Yes, he has great talents.

HLESTAKOV: Very good, very good. I'll see about it. . . . I'll speak to . . . I have hopes . . . that can all be done; yes, yes. . . . (*Turning to* BOBCHINSKY.) Haven't *you* something to say to me?

BOBCHINSKY: Why, yes, I have a very humble petition.

HLESTAKOV: Well, what about?

BOBCHINSKY: I humbly beg you, when you return to Petersburg, to say to all those various grandees, senators, and admirals, "Your Grace," or, "Your Excellency, there lives in such-and-such a town a certain Petr Ivanovich Bobchinsky." Just tell them that there is such a person as Petr Ivanovich Bobchinsky.

HLESTAKOV: Very well.

BOBCHINSKY: And likewise, if you should meet the tsar, just say to him, "Your Imperial Majesty, in such-and-such a town there lives a certain Petr Ivanovich Bobchinsky."

HLESTAKOV: Very well.

DOBCHINSKY: Excuse me for troubling you with my presence.

BOBCHINSKY: Excuse me for troubling you with my presence.

HLESTAKOV: That's all right! That's all right! It was a pleasure. (*He shows them out.*)

SCENE VIII

HLESTAKOV, *alone*

HLESTAKOV: There are a good many functionaries here. And, by the way, it strikes me that they take me for an important government official. I really threw dust in their eyes yesterday. What foolishness! I believe I'll write all about it to Tryapichkin in Petersburg; he'll write a little satire and take them off first-rate. Hey, Osip! Bring me paper and ink. (OSIP *glances in at the door, saying,* "Right away.") And if Tryapichkin ever gets his tooth into anybody, let that man look out! He won't spare his own father for the sake of a lampoon, and he likes money, too. However, these officials are good fellows; it's a great point in their favor that they lent me money. I might as well see how much I've got. Here's three hundred from the Judge; three hundred from the Postmaster, six hundred, seven hundred, eight hundred. . . . What a greasy note! Eight hundred, nine hundred! Oho! more than a thousand! . . . Now, then, captain, just let me get at you now! We'll see who's who!

SCENE IX

HLESTAKOV, *and* OSIP *with ink and paper*

HLESTAKOV: Well, you blockhead, do you see how they receive and entertain me? (*He begins to write.*)

OSIP: Yes, thank God! Only do you want me to tell you something, Ivan Alexandrovich?

HLESTAKOV: What?

OSIP: Get away from here! By Heaven, it's time!

HLESTAKOV (*writing*): What nonsense! Why?

OSIP: Because. Deuce take 'em all! We've bummed two days here, and that's enough. Why tie up with 'em any longer? Spit on 'em! Before you know it some one else may arrive. . . . Yes, Ivan Alexandrovich, by Heavens! There are some splendid horses here—they'd give us a fine ride.

HLESTAKOV (*writing*): No, I'd like to stay here a little longer. Wait till to-morrow.

OSIP: But why to-morrow? Good God, let's skip, Ivan Alexandrovich! Although it's a great honor for you, all the same you know that we'd better be off quick; they've really taken you for some one else. . . . And your dad will be peeved because you've dawdled so long. Really, we'd have a grand ride! They'd furnish you tiptop horses here.

HLESTAKOV (*writing*): Well, all right. But first take this letter and get an order for post horses. And see to it that they're good horses! Tell the drivers that I'll give them a ruble apiece if they'll bowl along as if I were a special courier and sing songs! (*He continues writing.*) I imagine Tryapichkin will die laughing. . . .

OSIP: I'll send the letter by the house servant, sir; but I'd better attend to our packing to save time.

HLESTAKOV (*writing*): All right, only bring me a candle.

OSIP (*goes out and speaks behind the scene*): Hey, listen, my boy! Take this letter to the post office and tell the Postmaster to frank it; and have them send my master their best troika of post horses; tell 'em my master won't be paying the fee, because it's at the government's expense. And tell 'em to look lively or the master'll be angry. Wait, the letter isn't ready yet.

HLSETAKOV (*continuing to write*): I'm curious to know whether he lives on Post Office Street or Gorokhovaya Street. He likes to change his lodgings frequently without paying up. I'll take a chance on addressing him at Post Office Street. (*He folds up the letter and addresses it.*)

(OSIP *brings in a candle.* HLESTAKOV *seals the letter. At the same time the voice of* DERZHIMORDA *is heard outside.*)

DERZHIMORDA: Where're you going, whiskers? I tell you I can't admit anybody.

HLESTAKOV (*handing* OSIP *the letter*): There, take it away.

Voices of MERCHANTS: Let us in, please! You can't refuse; we've come on business.

DERZHIMORDA: Go away! Go away! He's not receiving; he's asleep. (*The noise increases.*)

HLESTAKOV: What's going on there, Osip? Go see what the noise is about.

OSIP (*looking out of the window*): Some merchants want to come in, but the policemen won't let 'em. They're waving some papers; they really want to see you.

HLESTAKOV (*going to the window*): What do you want, my good men?

Voices of MERCHANTS: We appeal to your kindness. Give orders to receive our petitions, your Honor.

HLESTAKOV: Let 'em in, let 'em in! Let 'em come. Osip, tell 'em to come in. (OSIP *goes out.*)

HLESTAKOV (*accepts the petitions through the window, unrolls one of them and reads*): "To his Honorable Excellency the Minister of Finance from the merchant Abdulin." . . . What the devil! There's no such rank!

SCENE X

HLESTAKOV, *and the* MERCHANTS, *who carry a basket of wine and loaf sugar*

HLESTAKOV: What do you want, my good men?

MERCHANTS: We humbly implore your favor.

HLESTAKOV: But what do you want?

MERCHANTS: Don't ruin us, sir! We are suffering insults for no cause at all.

HLESTAKOV: From whom?

ONE OF THE MERCHANTS: All from the chief of police of this town. There never was such a Chief of Police, your Honor. He invents such insults as are beyond description. He has ruined us with billeting, until we want to hang ourselves. And his behavior is simply awful. He'll seize a man by the beard and say, "Ha, you Tatar!" By Heaven, he does! It isn't as though we hadn't shown him respect; we always do the regular thing, giving him cloth for his dear wife's clothes and his daughter's—we don't object to that. But, bless you, that's not enough for him; oh, no! He walks into the shop and takes anything he can lay his hands on. He'll see a piece of cloth and say, "Hey, my dear fellow, that's a fine piece of cloth; just send it over to me." Well, you take it over—and there's pretty close to forty yards in the piece.

HLESTAKOV: Is it possible? Why, what a swindler he is!

MERCHANTS: By Heaven, nobody can remember such a chief of police. You have to hide everything in the shop when you catch sight of him. And that's not saying that he takes only delicacies; oh, no! Dried prunes that have been lying in the barrel seven years and my own clerks wouldn't eat, he'll put away by the pocketful. His name day's St. Anthony's,* and on that day we take him seems like everything he needs; but no, we've got to keep it up; he says St. Onufry's his name day too. What can we do? We bring him stuff on St. Onufry's also.

HLESTAKOV: He's a regular highwayman!

MERCHANT: I'll say! And just try to say no to him, and he'll quarter a whole regiment on you. And if you object, he'll have the doors locked on you. "I'm not going to subject you to corporal punishment," he says, "or put you to the torture—that's forbidden by law," he says; "but you're going to eat salted herrings, my man." †

HLESTAKOV: Oh, what a swindler! Why, he ought to be sent to Siberia!

MERCHANTS: We don't care where your Honor packs him off to; any place'll do so long as it's far from us. Don't scorn our bread and salt, father: we beg to present you with this loaf sugar and this basket of wine.

HLESTAKOV: No, don't think of such a thing; I accept absolutely no bribes. But, for instance, if you should propose to lend me three hundred rubles—well, that would be another matter: I can accept loans.

MERCHANTS: Please do, your Honor! (*Taking out money.*) But why three hundred? You had better take five; only help us!

HLESTAKOV: Thanks. I have nothing to say against a loan; I'll take it.

MERCHANTS (*handing him the money on a silver tray*): And please take the tray with it.

HLESTAKOV: Well, you can throw the tray in.

MERCHANTS (*bowing*): And for once you might take the sugar.

---

* In Russia the day of the saint for whom a person is named is a family holiday.

† "To produce excessive thirst. This indirect form of torture was employed, to extort confession, by the secret police."—Sykes.

HLESTAKOV: Oh, no, I never take any bribes. . . .

OSIP: Your Honor, why not take it? Do! Everything comes in good on the road. Just hand over the sugar and the sack. Give us everything; it'll all come in useful. What's that—a rope? Give us the rope, too; a rope is useful in traveling; the wagon may break down or something, and you'll have to tie it up.

MERCHANTS: Just do us the favor, your Grace! If you don't help us out as we ask you to, we shan't know what to do: we might as well hang ourselves.

HLESTAKOV: Without fail! Without fail! I'll do my best. (*The merchants go out.*)

A WOMAN'S *Voice* (*outside*): No, don't you dare refuse to admit me! I'll complain to him himself! Stop shoving so hard!

HLESTAKOV: Who's there? (*Going to the window.*) What's the matter, my good woman?

Voices of TWO WOMEN: We beseech your favor, sir! Please hear us, your Honor!

HLESTAKOV (*out of the window*): Let her in.

SCENE XI

HLESTAKOV, *the* LOCKSMITH'S WIFE, *and the* SERGEANT'S WIDOW

LOCKSMITH'S WIFE (*bowing down to his feet*): I implore your favor. . . .

SERGEANT'S WIDOW: I implore your favor. . . .

HLESTAKOV: Who are you, my good women?

SERGEANT'S WIDOW: I'm the widow of Sergeant Ivanov.

LOCKSMITH'S WIFE: I'm the wife of a locksmith of the town, Fevronya Petrova Poshlepkin, sir.

HLESTAKOV: Wait; speak one at a time. What do you want?

LOCKSMITH'S WIFE: I implore your aid against the Chief of Police! May God send him every evil! May his children, and he, the swindler, and his uncles and his aunts, prosper in nothing they ever do!

HLESTAKOV: Why?

LOCKSMITH'S WIFE: He sent my husband away as a soldier, and it wasn't our turn, the scoundrel! And it's against the law, too, he being a married man.

HLESTAKOV: How could he do that?

LOCKSMITH'S WIFE: He did it, the scoundrel, he did it! May God smite him in this world and the next! May every misfortune visit him and his aunt, too, if he has one, and if his father's living, the rascal, may he croak or choke himself forever—such a scoundrel he is! He ought to have taken the tailor's son, who's a drunkard anyway; but his parents made him a handsome present; so he jumped on the son of Mrs. Panteleyev, the shopkeeper; but Mrs. Panteleyev sent his wife three pieces of cloth, and so he came to me. "What good's your husband to you?" says he. "He's no use to you." As if I didn't know whether he's any use or not; that's my business—the scoundrel! "He's a thief," says he; "although he hasn't stolen anything yet, it's all the same," he says; "he will; and anyway he'll be sent as a recruit next year." How can I manage without my husband—the scoundrel! I'm a weak woman, and you're a villain! May none of your relatives ever see the light of God! And if you have a mother-in-law, may she—!

HLESTAKOV: All right, all right. (*He shows the old woman out. Then to the other woman.*) And you, now?

LOCKSMITH'S WIFE (*going*): Don't forget, honored sir! Be merciful to me!

SERGEANT'S WIDOW: I've come to complain against the Chief of Police, sir.

HLESTAKOV: Well, what about? Put it in a few words.

SERGEANT'S WIDOW: He beat me up, sir!

HLESTAKOV: How?

SERGEANT'S WIDOW: By mistake, your Honor! Some of our peasant women were fighting in the market, but the police didn't get there soon enough, so they nabbed me, and reported me: I couldn't sit down for two days.

HLESTAKOV: Well, what's to be done about it, now?

SERGEANT'S WIDOW: Of course, there's nothing to be done now. But you can make him pay damages for making the mistake. I can't turn my back on my own luck, and the money would help me a lot just now.

HLESTAKOV: Well, well, run along, run along; I'll see to it. (*Several hands containing petitions are thrust through the window.*) What next? (*Approaching the window.*) I don't want them! I don't want them! There's no use! There's no use! (*Going away.*) They make me tired, deuce take 'em! Don't let 'em in, Osip!

OSIP (*shouting out the window*): Go away, go away! He hasn't time now! Come back to-morrow!

(*The door opens and there appears a strange figure in a frieze overcoat, unshaven, with a swollen lip and bandaged cheek; behind him several others appear in perspective.*)

OSIP: Get out, get out! Where'd you come from?

(*He gives the first one a push in the belly and forces his own way out into the passage with him, slamming the door behind him.*)

SCENE XII

HLESTAKOV, *and* MARYA ANTONOVNA

MARYA ANTONOVNA: Oh!

HLESTAKOV: What are you afraid of, young lady?

MARYA ANTONOVNA: No, I wasn't frightened.

HLESTAKOV (*posing*): It is most gratifying to me, young lady, that you should take me for a man who . . . May I be so bold as to ask you where you were going?

MARYA ANTONOVNA: Well, really, I wasn't going anywhere.

HLESTAKOV: And why weren't you, if I may ask?

MARYA ANTONOVNA: I thought mamma might be here. . . .

HLESTAKOV: No, I'd like to know why you weren't going anywhere.

MARYA ANTONOVNA: I've disturbed you. You were engaged with important matters.

HLESTAKOV (*posing*): Your eyes are more important than mere business. . . . You couldn't possibly disturb me, not in any manner whatsoever; on the contrary, you only bring me pleasure.

MARYA ANTONOVNA: You're talking in Petersburg style.

HLESTAKOV: To such a beautiful creature as you. Dare I be so happy as to offer you a chair? But no, you need, not a chair but a throne.

MARYA ANTONOVNA: Really, I don't know . . . I think I ought to be going. (*She sits down.*)

HLESTAKOV: What a beautiful fichu you have on!

MARYA ANTONOVNA: You men are flatterers; you just want to laugh at us provincials.

HLESTAKOV: How I should like to be your fichu, young lady, that I might embrace your lily-white neck.

MARYA ANTONOVNA: I'm sure I don't know what you're talking about: a little fichu. . . . What strange weather we're having to-day!

HLESTAKOV: But your lips, young lady, are better than any kind of weather!

MARYA ANTONOVNA: You keep talking like that! . . . I'd better ask you to write me some verses in my autograph album, as a souvenir. You surely know a lot of them.

HLESTAKOV: For your sake, young lady, I'll do anything you want. Command me, what sort of verses do you wish?

MARYA ANTONOVNA: Oh, any kind . . . such as . . . good ones . . . and new.

HLESTAKOV: But what are verses! I know a lot of them.

MARYA ANTONOVNA: Just say over the kind you're going to write for me.

HLESTAKOV: Why say them? I know them without doing that.

MARYA ANTONOVNA: I'm so fond of poetry.

HLESTAKOV: Well, I know a lot of different poems. For instance, I might write this for you:

> O man, who in thine hour of grief
> Against thy God in vain complainest. . . . *

And there are others. . . . I can't recall them now; however, that's all right. Instead I had better present you with my love, which your eyes have . . . (*Moving his chair nearer.*)

MARYA ANTONOVNA: Love! I don't understand love! . . . I have never known what love is. . . . (*She moves her chair away.*)

HLESTAKOV: Why do you move your chair away? It would be better for us to sit close together.

MARYA ANTONOVNA (*moving away*): Why close together? We're as well off at a distance.

HLESTAKOV (*moving nearer*): Why at a distance? We're as well off nearer.

MARYA ANTONOVNA (*moving away*): But why is that?

HLESTAKOV (*moving nearer*): It just seems to you that we're close; but you ought to imagine we're far apart. How happy I should be, young lady, if I could only hold you in my embrace.

MARYA ANTONOVNA (*looking out the window*): I wonder what that was that flew by. Was it a magpie or some other bird?

HLESTAKOV (*kissing her shoulder and looking out the window*): That was a magpie.

MARYA ANTONOVNA (*rising in indignation*): No, this is too much! . . . Such impudence! . . .

HLESTAKOV (*detaining her*): Forgive me, young lady, I did it from love, only from love.

MARYA ANTONOVNA: You consider me only a common provincial girl. . . . (*She tries to get away.*)

HLESTAKOV (*continues to detain her*): From love, truly, only from love. I was only joking, Marya Antonovna; don't be angry. I'm ready to beg forgiveness on my knees. (*He falls upon his knees.*) Forgive me, please forgive me! You see, I'm on my knees.

---

* The opening lines of an ode by Lomonosov (1708?-1765). Hlestakov recalls a scrap of an old-fashioned poet that he learned at school! (Adapted from Sykes.)

SCENE XIII

The same and ANNA ANDREYEVNA

ANNA ANDREYEVNA (*seeing* HLESTAKOV *on his knees*): Oh, what a scene!

HLESTAKOV (*rising*): Oh, the deuce!

ANNA ANDREYEVNA (*to her daughter*): What does this mean, young lady? What sort of behavior is this?

MARYA ANTONOVNA: Mamma, I . . .

ANNA ANDREYEVNA: Go away at once, do you hear? Go away, go away! Don't you dare show yourself before my eyes. (MARYA ANTONOVNA *goes out in tears.*) Pardon me, but I confess I was carried away by astonishment. . . .

HLESTAKOV (*aside*): She's also rather appetizing, not half bad-looking. (*Throwing himself upon his knees.*) Madam, you see, I am consumed with love.

ANNA ANDREYEVNA: What, on your knees? Oh, please get up. The floor is anything but clean.

HLESTAKOV: No, upon my knees, absolutely upon my knees, I wish to know my fate. Is it life or death?

ANNA ANDREYEVNA: I beg your pardon, but I still don't entirely understand your words. If I am not mistaken, you are declaring your sentiments regarding my daughter.

HLESTAKOV: No, I am in love with you. My life hangs by a hair. If you do not crown my constant love, then I am unworthy of earthly existence. With flames in my bosom I beseech your hand.

ANNA ANDREYEVNA: Permit me to remark that I am—well, as they say . . . married.

HLESTAKOV: That's nothing! In love that makes no difference. Even Karamzin says, "The laws condemn it." * We shall flee to the shade of the streams! . . . Your hand, I ask your hand.

SCENE XIV

The same and MARYA ANTONOVNA, *who comes in running*

MARYA ANTONOVNA: Mamma, papa says for you to . . . (*Seeing* HLESTAKOV *on his knees, and exclaiming.*) Oh, what a scene!

ANNA ANDREYEVNA: Well, what's the matter with you! What did *you* come in for? What flightiness! She runs in like a cat in a fit!

* "Quoted from some verses in the romance, *Bornholm Island*, by Karamzin (1766-1826)."—Sykes.

Well, what have you found that's so surprising? What have you thought up? Really, you act like a three-year-old child. No one in the world would ever think she was eighteen years old. I don't know when you'll have any more sense, or when you'll behave like a well-brought-up girl, or when you'll know what good principles and propriety are.

MARYA ANTONOVNA (*through her tears*): Really, mamma, I didn't know . . .

ANNA ANDREYEVNA: You always have wheels in your head; you pattern after Lyapkin-Tyapkin's daughters! Much good it does you to imitate them! You needn't copy them. There are other models for you—you have your mother, for example. That's the example you ought to follow!

HLESTAKOV (*seizing the daughter's hand*): Anna Andreyevna, do not oppose our felicity, bless our constant love!

ANNA ANDREYEVNA (*astonished*): And so you're in love with *her?*

HLESTAKOV: Decide! Is it life or death?

ANNA ANDREYEVNA: There, you see, you little fool, you see: all on your account, you rubbish, our guest was on his knees; and you had to run in like a chicken with its head off. I really ought to refuse my consent: you're unworthy such good fortune.

MARYA ANTONOVNA: I won't do it again, mamma; really, I won't do it again.

SCENE XV

The same and the CHIEF OF POLICE, *who enters out of breath*

CHIEF OF POLICE: Your Excellency, don't ruin me, don't ruin me!

HLESTAKOV: What's the matter?

CHIEF OF POLICE: The merchants have been complaining to your Excellency. I assure you on my honor that not half of what they say is true. They're the ones who cheat and overreach the people. The sergeant's widow lied to you, saying I'd flogged her; she's lying, by God, she's lying! She flogged herself.

HLESTAKOV: Damn the sergeant's widow; I've nothing to do with her!

CHIEF OF POLICE: Don't believe it, don't believe it! . . . They're all liars! Not even a baby would believe them. They're known for liars all over town. And so far as swindling goes, I venture to inform you that they are swindlers such as the earth has never produced before.

ANNA ANDREYEVNA: Do you know the honor that Ivan Alexandrovich has done us? He is asking for our daughter's hand.

CHIEF OF POLICE: What in the world! . . . You've gone crazy, my dear! Don't be angry, your Excellency; she's a little bit off, and her mother was the same.

HLESTAKOV: But I actually am asking for her hand. I'm in love.

CHIEF OF POLICE: I can't believe it, your Excellency!

ANNA ANDREYEVNA: But when you're told so!

HLESTAKOV: I'm not joking you. . . . I may go mad from love.

CHIEF OF POLICE: I don't dare believe it; I'm unworthy of such an honor.

HLESTAKOV: Yes, if you do not agree to give me Marya Antonovna's hand, then I'm ready to do the devil knows what. . . .

CHIEF OF POLICE: I can't believe it! Your Excellency is having his joke!

ANNA ANDREYEVNA: Oh, what a blockhead you are! When he's explaining it to you?

CHIEF OF POLICE: I can't believe it!

HLESTAKOV: Give her, give her to me! I'm a desperate man, ready for anything: when I shoot myself, you'll be put on trial!

CHIEF OF POLICE: Oh, my God! I'm really not to blame, in intention or in fact! Please don't be angry! Just act as your Honor wishes! My poor head, really . . . I don't know myself what's going on. I've made a bigger blockhead of myself than ever.

ANNA ANDREYEVNA: Well, give 'em your blessing!

(HLESTAKOV *approaches him with* MARYA ANTONOVNA.)

CHIEF OF POLICE: May God bless you! It's not my fault! (HLESTAKOV *kisses* MARYA ANTONOVNA. *The* CHIEF OF POLICE *watches them.*) What the devil! They really are! (*Wiping his eyes.*) They're kissing! Holy Saints, they're kissing! They're actually engaged! (*Shouting and prancing with joy.*) Hey, Anton! Hey, Anton! Aha, Police Chief! That's the way it's turned out!

SCENE XVI

The same and OSIP

OSIP: The horses are ready.

HLESTAKOV: Oh, all right. . . . In a minute.

CHIEF OF POLICE: What, sir? Are you leaving?

HLESTAKOV: Yes, I am.

CHIEF OF POLICE: But when? . . . That is . . . you hinted something about a wedding, didn't you?

HLESTAKOV: Oh, as to that . . . it's only for a minute—just a day with my uncle. He's a rich old man—and to-morrow I'll be back.

CHIEF OF POLICE: We dare not detain you and we hope for your prosperous return.

HLESTAKOV: Why, of course, of course, I'll be right back. Good-by, my love. . . . No, I simply cannot express myself! Good-by, my darling! (*He kisses her hand.*)

CHIEF OF POLICE: But don't you need anything for traveling? You were somewhat short of money, weren't you?

HLESTAKOV: Oh, no, what for? (*Upon reflection.*) However, if you wish.

CHIEF OF POLICE: How much would you like?

HLESTAKOV: Well, you gave me two hundred, that is, not two hundred, but four—I don't want to profit by your mistake—so perhaps you'd be willing to let me have as much again, to make an even eight hundred.

CHIEF OF POLICE: At once! (*He takes it from his pocketbook.*) Fortunately I have it in brand-new bills.

HLESTAKOV: Ah, yes. (*He takes the notes and looks at them.*) That's fine. They say that new notes bring good luck.

CHIEF OF POLICE: Just so, sir.

HLESTAKOV: Good-by, Anton Antonovich! I'm much obliged for your hospitality. I confess from the bottom of my heart, I've never had such a kind reception. Good-by, Anna Andreyevna! Good-by, my darling Marya Antonovna! (*They go out.*)

(*Voices behind the scenes.*)

HLESTAKOV's *Voice:* Good-by, Marya Antonovna, my soul's angel!

Voice of the CHIEF OF POLICE: What's this? You're going by the public post?

HLESTAKOV's *Voice:* Yes, I'm used to it. Springs give me the headache.

DRIVER's *Voice:* Whoa!

Voice of the CHIEF OF POLICE: Then at least let me spread something on the seat: a rug, for instance. Won't you let me give you a little rug?

HLESTAKOV's *Voice:* No, what for? That's needless; still, you might let them bring a rug.

Voice of the CHIEF OF POLICE: Hey, Avdotya! Run to the storeroom and bring out the best rug—the Persian one with the blue ground. Hurry!

DRIVER's *Voice:* Whoa!

Voice of the CHIEF OF POLICE: When may we expect you back?

HLESTAKOV's *Voice:* To-morrow or the day after.

OSIP's *Voice:* Ah, is that the rug? Well, give it here; fold it like this. Now put some hay on this side.

DRIVER'S *Voice:* Whoa!

OSIP'S *Voice:* Here on this side! Here! That'll do! Good! That'll be fine. (*Slapping his hand on the rug.*) Now, sit down, your Honor!

HLESTAKOV'S *Voice:* Good-by, Anton Antonovich!

Voice of the CHIEF OF POLICE: Good-by, your Excellency!

WOMEN'S *Voices:* Good-by, Ivan Alexandrovich!

HLESTAKOV'S *Voice:* Good-by, mamma!

DRIVER'S *Voice:* Giddap, my beauties! (*The harness bells jingle; the curtain falls.*)

ACT V

The same room

SCENE I

The CHIEF OF POLICE, ANNA ANDREYEVNA, *and* MARYA ANTONOVNA

CHIEF OF POLICE: Well, Anna Andreyevna, what about it? Would you ever have expected it? What a rich prize, hang it all! Now, admit it candidly: you never even dreamed of such luck! From being a mere police chief's wife suddenly to . . . oh, the deuce! . . . to make connections with such a devil as this!

ANNA ANDREYEVNA: Not at all; I knew it all the time. It seems wonderful to you, because you're an ordinary man and have never seen decent people.

CHIEF OF POLICE: I'm a decent man myself, dear. On the other hand, really, when you think of it, Anna Andreyevna, what fine birds you and I have become! Ha, Anna Andreyevna? We'll fly high, deuce take it! Just wait, now I'll pepper those guys for presenting petitions and denunciations! Hey, who's there? (*A policeman comes in.*) Oh, it's you, Ivan Karpovich. Call the merchants in, my boy. I'll give it to them, the rascals! To complain about *me!* Nothing but a damned bunch of Jews! Just wait, sweethearts! Up to date I've merely warmed your breeches, but now I'll tan your whole hides! Write down the name of every man who came to peach on me, and, above all, the scribblers who fixed up their petitions for them. And you can announce so they'll all know it, what an honor God has bestowed on the Chief of Police, who is marrying his daughter to no ordinary man, but to one whose like can't be found on earth, a man who can do everything, everything, everything! Announce it so they'll all know it. Shout it to the whole population! Ring the bells, dammit! This is a regular holiday. (*The policeman goes out.*) That's the way, Anna

Andreyevna, huh? What'll we do now, where shall we live: here or in Petersburg?

ANNA ANDREYEVNA: In Petersburg, of course. How could we stay here!

CHIEF OF POLICE: Well, if it's to be Petersburg, so be it; but it wouldn't be so bad here. And I suppose the police business may go to hell, huh, Anna Andreyevna?

ANNA ANDREYEVNA: Of course; what's a police job!

CHIEF OF POLICE: Don't you think, Anna Andreyevna, I may now land a swell title? He's chummy with all the ministers and goes to the Palace, so he may get me promoted in time to a generalship. What do you think, Anna Andreyevna, may I get to be a general?

ANNA ANDREYEVNA: Sure, of course you may.

CHIEF OF POLICE: It's damned nice to be a general! They hang decorations across your breast! Which ribbon is better, Anna Andreyevna, the red or the blue?

ANNA ANDREYEVNA: Of course the blue is best.

CHIEF OF POLICE: Eh? So that's what you fancy. Well, the red's nice, too. Why do I want to be a general? Because if it happens that you travel anywhere, messengers and adjutants gallop ahead everywhere, shouting, "Horses!" And at the posting stations they won't give any to any one else; all have to wait: all those titular councilors, captains, police chiefs—and you don't give a snap of your fingers. You dine somewhere at a governor's, and there a police chief has to stand! He, he, he! (*He laughs himself into a perspiration.*) That's what's so attractive, damn it!

ANNA ANDREYEVNA: You always like everything vulgar. You must remember that we've got to change our whole manner of living, that your acquaintances won't be like the dog fancier Judge with whom you course hares, or like Zemlyanika; on the contrary, your acquaintances will be from the most refined society, counts and swells. . . . Though I'm really scared on your account: you'll let slip occasionally some word that simply isn't heard in polite society.

CHIEF OF POLICE: What of it? A word doesn't hurt.

ANNA ANDREYEVNA: It was all right while you were a police chief; but in Petersburg life will be quite different.

CHIEF OF POLICE: Yes; they say that there are two kinds of fish there, sea-eels and sparlings, which simply make your mouth water when you begin to eat.

ANNA ANDREYEVNA: He's always thinking about fish! I want to be sure that our house is the swellest in the capital, and I want such an odor of ambergris in my drawing-room that there'll be no going into it: you'll simply have to shut your eyes. (*She shuts her eyes and sniffs.*) Oh, how nice!

SCENE II

The same and the MERCHANTS

CHIEF OF POLICE: Ah, how are you, you flock of hawks!

MERCHANTS (*bowing*): We wish you good health, sir!

CHIEF OF POLICE: Well, darlings, how are you? How's trade, eh? What, you tea-swilling cloth-stretchers, you'll complain, will you? You arch-rascals, you dirty brutes, you swollen swindlers, you'll complain, will you? Well, did you get much? They thought they'd have me thrown in the jug! . . . Do you know, I'll swear by seven devils and one witch that . . .

ANNA ANDREYEVNA: Oh, good Heavens, Antosha, what words you use!

CHIEF OF POLICE (*greatly displeased*): Words don't matter now. Do you know that that very official to whom you complained is marrying my daughter? Do you? What d'you say now? Now I'll fix you! . . . You deceive people. . . . You make a contract with the government and swindle it out of a hundred thousand by supplying rotten cloth, and then you donate twenty yards and expect to be rewarded for it! And if they found it out, you'd catch it! . . . He struts along, belly foremost: he's a merchant; nobody must touch him! "We don't give way even to the nobility," he says. As for a nobleman . . . Bah, you pigs' mugs! . . . A nobleman studies the sciences; and if they beat him at school, it's to some purpose, so that he'll learn something useful. But what about you? You begin with rascalities, and you're beaten by the master because you don't know how to cheat. While still little brats, before you know your Lord's Prayer, you give short measure; and when you've developed a belly and lined your pockets with money, how you do put on airs! Oh, you're wonders, I'll say! Because you empty sixteen samovars a day, you put on airs, do you? I spit on you and your conceit!

MERCHANTS (*bowing*): We're at fault, Anton Antonovich!

CHIEF OF POLICE: Complain, will you? But who helped you swindle when you built the bridge and charged twenty thousand for lumber when you didn't use a hundred rubles' worth? I helped you, you old billy goat! * Have you forgotten that? If I had peached on you for that, I could have sent you to Siberia. What d'you say, ha?

ONE OF THE MERCHANTS: God knows we're guilty, Anton Antono-

* "At the date of the play, only the lower classes wore beards."—Sykes.

vich! The devil misled us. We swear never to complain again. Demand any satisfaction you please, only don't be angry!

CHIEF OF POLICE: Don't be angry! And now you're wallowing at my feet. And why? Because I've got the upper hand; but if you had even the least advantage, you scum, you'd trample me in the very mud, and roll a log over me.

MERCHANTS (*bowing to his feet*): Don't ruin us, Anton Antonovich!

CHIEF OF POLICE: "Don't ruin us!" Now it's "Don't ruin us!" But what was it before? I could . . . (*Waving his hand.*) Well, God forgive you! That'll do! I'm not vindictive; only see that you look sharp from now on! I'm not marrying my daughter to any ordinary noble: let your congratulations be . . . d'you understand? Don't try to wriggle out of it with a chunk of dried sturgeon or a loaf of sugar. . . . Now, go to the devil! (*The* MERCHANTS *go out.*)

SCENE III

The same, AMMOS FEDOROVICH, ARTEMY FILIPPOVICH, *and later* RASTAKOVSKY

AMMOS FEDOROVICH (*still in the door*): Can I believe the rumors, Anton Antonovich? Has this unusual good luck really struck you?

ARTEMY FILIPPOVICH: I have the honor to congratulate you upon your unusual good fortune. I rejoiced with all my soul when I heard about it. (*He goes to kiss* ANNA ANDREYEVNA'S *hand.*) Anna Andreyevna! (*He goes to kiss* MARYA ANTONOVNA'S *hand.*) Marya Antonovna!

RASTKOVSKY (*entering*): I congratulate Anton Antonovich! May God prolong your life and that of the new pair, and give you a numerous posterity of grandchildren and great-grandchildren! Anna Andreyevna! (*Going to kiss her hand.*) Marya Antonovna! (*Going to kiss her hand.*)

SCENE IV

The same, KOROBKIN *and his wife, and* LYULYUKOV

KOROBKIN: I have the honor to congratulate Anton Antonovich! Anna Andreyevna! (*Going to kiss her hand.*) Marya Antonovna! (*Going to kiss her hand.*)

KOROBKIN'S WIFE: I congratulate you from my soul, Anna Andreyevna, upon your new happiness!

LYULYUKOV: I have the honor to congratulate you, Anna Andreyevna. (*He goes to kiss her hand, then turning towards the spectators, he makes a clicking sound with his tongue with an air of bravado.)* Marya Antonovna, I have the honor to congratulate you! *(He goes to kiss her hand and turns to the spectators with the same bravado.)*

SCENE V

A number of guests in frock coats and swallowtails come up first to kiss the hand of ANNA ANDREYEVNA, *saying her name, then to* MARYA ANTONOVNA, *saying hers.* BOBCHINSKY *and* DOBCHINSKY *push their way forward.*

BOBCHINSKY: I have the honor to congratulate you!

DOBCHINSKY: Anton Antonovich, I have the honor to congratulate you!

BOBCHINSKY: Upon this prosperous event!

DOBCHINSKY: Anna Andreyevna!

BOBCHINSKY: Anna Andreyevna! *(Both go up to kiss her hand at the same time and knock their heads together.)*

DOBCHINSKY: Marya Antonovna! *(He goes to kiss her hand.)* I have the honor to congratulate you. You will be very, very happy; you will walk in cloth of gold and eat all sorts of delicate soups, and pass your time very entertainingly.

BOBCHINSKY *(interrupting)*: Marya Antonovna, I have the honor to congratulate you! May God give you all kinds of riches and gold and a baby boy no bigger than that! *(Showing with his hand.)* So small he can sit on the palm of your hand, yes, ma'am; and all the time he'll cry wa, wa, wa!

SCENE VI

Still more guests come to kiss the ladies' hands, among them LUKA LUKICH *and his* WIFE

LUKA LUKICH: I have the honor. . . .

LUKA LUKICH'S WIFE: *(running forward)*: I congratulate you, Anna Andreyevna! *(They kiss.)* I was so delighted, truly. They told me, "Anna Andreyevna is marrying off her daughter." "Oh, my goodness," I thought to myself; and I was so delighted that I said to my husband, "Listen, Luky-duky, here's a new happiness for Anna Andreyevna!" "Well," I thought, "thank God!" And I said to him, "I'm so beside myself with joy that I'm burning with impatience to declare it personally to Anna Andreyevna." . . . "Oh, good heavens!" I thought to myself, "Anna Andreyevna was just waiting for a good match for her daughter, and now see what fate has done: it has all happened exactly as she wished." And truly, I was so glad that I couldn't speak. I wept and wept; why, I fairly sobbed. Luka Lukich even said, "Nastenka, what are you sobbing about?" "Luky-duky," I said, "I don't know, myself; the tears are just flowing in a stream."

CHIEF OF POLICE: I humbly beg you to be seated, ladies and gentlemen! Hey, Mishka, bring in some more chairs here! (*The guests sit down.*)

SCENE VII

The same, the POLICE CAPTAIN, *and* SERGEANTS OF POLICE

POLICE CAPTAIN: I have the honor to congratulate you, your Honor, and to wish you prosperity and long life!

CHIEF OF POLICE: Thanks, thanks! I beg you to sit down, gentlemen! (*The guests sit down.*)

AMMOS FEDOROVICH: Now please tell us, Anton Antonovich, how all this started, the whole thing, step by step.

CHIEF OF POLICE: The course of the affair was extraordinary: he was kind enough to make the proposal in person.

ANNA ANDREYEVNA: Very respectfully, and in the most refined manner. He put everything extraordinarily well. "It's only out of respect for your virtues, Anna Andreyevna," he said. And he's such a handsome, well-bred man, of the most aristocratic manners. "Believe me, Anna Andreyevna," he said, "my life isn't worth a kopek; I'm doing this only because I respect your rare qualities."

MARYA ANTONOVNA: Why, mamma, he said that to me!

ANNA ANDREYEVNA: Stop it! You don't know anything about it. Don't mix into everything! "I'm astonished, Anna Andreyevna," he says. Then he launched forth into the most flattering words . . . and when I wanted to say, "We really don't dare hope for such an honor," he suddenly fell upon his knees and said in the most aristocratic style: "Anna Andreyevna, don't make me wretched! Please consent to reciprocate my feelings, or I shall let death end it all."

MARYA ANTONOVNA: Really, mamma, he said that about me. . . .

ANNA ANDREYEVNA: Yes, of course . . . it was about you, also. . . . I don't deny it at all.

CHIEF OF POLICE: As it was he frightened me; he said he would shoot himself. "I'll shoot myself, I'll shoot myself!" he said.

NUMEROUS GUESTS: Really, you don't say!

AMMOS FEDOROVICH: Well I declare!

LUKA LUKICH: It was surely fate that brought this to pass.

ARTEMY FILIPPOVICH: Not fate, old man, fate's too flighty a bird: his merits have done it. (*Aside.*) Luck always comes to such swine as he!

AMMOS FEDOROVICH: If you want him, I'll give you that pup you were bargaining for, Anton Antonovich.

CHIEF OF POLICE: No, I've no use for pups now.

AMMOS FEDOROVICH: Well, if you don't want him, we can agree on another dog.

KOROBKIN'S WIFE: Oh, Anna Andreyevna, how glad I am of your happiness! You simply can't imagine!

KOROBKIN: And where, if I may ask, is our eminent guest now? I heard that he had gone away for some reason.

CHIEF OF POLICE: Yes, he has left for one day, on a very important matter.

ANNA ANDREYEVNA: To see his uncle and ask his blessing.

CHIEF OF POLICE: To ask his blessing; but to-morrow . . . (*He sneezes, and is greeted by a din of good wishes.*) Thanks very much! But to-morrow he'll be back. . . . (*He sneezes again; renewed chorus of good wishes; the following people speak louder than the others.*)

POLICE CAPTAIN: We wish you good health, your Honor!

BOBCHINSKY: A hundred years and a sack of gold!

DOBCHINSKY: God prolong your days forever and ever!

ARTEMY FILIPPOVICH: May you croak!

KOROBKIN'S WIFE: The devil take you!

CHIEF OF POLICE: I humbly thank you! I wish you the same.

ANNA ANDREYEVNA: We're planning to live in Petersburg now. I confess that in this town there's an atmosphere that's too . . . well, countrified! . . . I confess it's very disagreeable. . . . And my husband—he'll be made a general there.

CHIEF OF POLICE: Yes, and I admit, ladies and gentlemen, deuce take it, that I'd like awfully to be a general.

LUKA LUKICH: God grant you may be!

RASTAKOVSKY: What is impossible for man is possible for God.

AMMOS FEDOROVICH: A big ship travels far.*

ARTEMY FILIPPOVICH: Your merits deserve the honor.

AMMOS FEDOROVICH (*aside*): That will be the limit, if they actually make him a general! A generalship will suit him like a saddle on a cow! But no, it's a far cry from this to that. There are men here more respectable than you that aren't generals yet.

ARTEMY FILIPPOVICH (*aside*): And so he's crawling into a general's boots! What the devil! But there's no telling; he may get to be a

* "Russian proverb."—Sykes.

general. The devil knows he's got conceit enough for it. (*Turning to him.*) Don't forget us then, Anton Antonovich.

AMMOS FEDOROVICH: And if anything should happen—for instance, some emergency in our affairs—don't deny us your patronage!

KOROBKIN: Next year I shall take my son to the capital to enter the government service. Please do us the favor to grant him your protection; be like a father to an orphan child.

CHIEF OF POLICE: I'm quite ready, for my part, to do what I can.

ANNA ANDREYEVNA: Antosha, you're always ready to make promises. In the first place, you'll have no time to think about that. How can you, and why should you, burden yourself with such promises?

CHIEF OF POLICE: Why not, my dear? Sometimes one can do something.

ANNA ANDREYEVNA: Of course one can; but one can't patronize all the small fry.

KOROBKIN'S WIFE: Do you hear how she's treating us?

A WOMAN GUEST: Yes, she was always like that. I know her. Let her sit at the table and she'll put her feet on it.*

SCENE VIII

The same and the POSTMASTER, *who enters out of breath, with an unsealed letter in his hand*

POSTMASTER: An astonishing thing, ladies and gentlemen! The official whom we took to be the government inspector, was not the inspector at all.

ALL: What—not the inspector?

POSTMASTER: Absolutely not; I've learned from this letter.

CHIEF OF POLICE: What's that? What's that? From what letter?

POSTMASTER: Why, from his own letter. They brought me a letter to the post office. I glanced at the address and saw, "Post Office Street." I was stupefied. "Well," I thought to myself, "he's surely found some irregularity in the post office and is notifying the authorities." So I took and opened it.

CHIEF OF POLICE: How did you dare?

POSTMASTER: I don't know; some supernatural power inspired me. I was about to call a messenger to dispatch it by express; but such curiosity as I have never felt before overcame me. I couldn't let it go; I simply couldn't! I was just drawn to open it. In one ear I seemed to hear, "Don't unseal it! You'll croak on the spot!" But in the other some demon kept whispering, "Open it, open it, open it!" And when I

* "Russian proverb."—Sykes.

pressed the wax, a fire ran through my veins; and when I unsealed it, I was frozen, by Heaven I was. My hands shook, and all went black before my eyes.

CHIEF OF POLICE: But how did you dare open the letter of such an august emissary?

POSTMASTER: But that's just the point; he ain't an emissary and he ain't august!

CHIEF OF POLICE: Well, what do you think he *is?*

POSTMASTER: A mere nobody; the devil knows what he is.

CHIEF OF POLICE (*testily*): What do you mean? How dare you call him a nobody and the devil knows who? I'll have you arrested!

POSTMASTER: Who? You?

CHIEF OF POLICE: Yes, I!

POSTMASTER: You ain't the size!

CHIEF OF POLICE: Don't you know that he is marrying my daughter, that I'm to be a dignitary myself, and that I can bundle you off to Siberia?

POSTMASTER: Oh, Anton Antonovich! What's Siberia? Siberia's far away. I'd better read you the letter. Ladies and gentlemen, shall I read the letter?

ALL: Read it, read it!

POSTMASTER (*reading*): "I hasten to inform you, my dear Tryapichkin, what wonders are happening to me. On the road I was cleaned out by an infantry captain, with the result that the innkeeper was going to have me jailed. Then all of a sudden, because of my Petersburg countenance and clothes, the whole town took me for a Governor-General. And now I'm living at the Police Chief's, enjoying myself, and flirting desperately with his wife and daughter. I haven't yet decided which one to begin with—I think the mother, because she seems to be ready to go the limit. Do you remember how hard up we used to be, and dined by being foxy; and how once a confectioner grabbed me by the collar because of some pastry we had eaten, telling him to charge it to the King of England? Now it's the other way round. Everybody lends me money, all I want. They're terrific freaks: you'd die laughing at them. I know you write articles; stick them in your contributions. In the first place, there's the Police Chief, as stupid as a gray jackass. . . ."

CHIEF OF POLICE: It can't be! It isn't there!

POSTMASTER (*showing the letter*): Read it yourself.

CHIEF OF POLICE (*reading*): "As a gray jackass." It can't be! You wrote that yourself!

POSTMASTER: How was I to write it?

ARTEMY FILIPPOVICH: Read it!

LUKA LUKICH: Read it!

POSTMASTER (*continuing his reading*): "the Police Chief—as stupid as a gray jackass. . . ."

CHIEF OF POLICE: "Oh, damn you! Do you have to repeat it? As if we didn't know it was there!

POSTMASTER (*continuing his reading*): Hm . . . hm . . . hm . . . hm . . . "a gray jackass. The Postmaster is also a nice chap. . . ." (*Stopping.*) Well, then he goes on to express himself rather indecently about me.

CHIEF OF POLICE: No, read it!

POSTMASTER: What for?

CHIEF OF POLICE: What the devil! If you're reading it, read it! Read it all!

ARTEMY FILIPPOVICH: Here, just let me read it. (*Putting on his spectacles and reading.*) "The Postmaster is the exact image of our department janitor, Mikheyev; and the rascal must be just such another old soak."

POSTMASTER (*to the spectators*): Well, he's a contemptible brat who needs a hiding; that's all!

ARTEMY FILIPPOVICH (*continuing*): "The Supervisor of Charitable Insti . . . tu . . . tu . . ." (*He begins to stammer.*)

KOROBKIN: Why are you stopping?

ARTEMY FILIPPOVICH: The writing is illegible . . . however, I can see he's a scamp.

KOROBKIN: Give it to me! I think I have better eyes. (*Taking hold of the letter.*)

ARTEMY FILIPPOVICH (*holding on to it*): No, we can skip that part; further on one can make it out.

KOROBKIN: Come on, I can do it.

ARTEMY FILIPPOVICH: If it has to be read, I'll do it myself: further on, really, it's quite legible.

POSTMASTER: No, read it all! So far everything has been read.

ALL: Give him the letter, Artemy Filippovich, give him the letter! (*To* KOROBKIN.) Read it!

ARTEMY FILIPPOVICH: All right. (*Giving the letter.*) Here, if you please . . . (*Covering part with his finger.*) Read from here on. (*All gather around him.*)

POSTMASTER: Read it, read it! Nonsense! Read it all!

KOROBKIN (*reading*): "The Supervisor of Charitable Institutions, Zemlyanika, is a regular pig in a nightcap."

ARTEMY FILIPPOVICH (*to the* SPECTATORS): It isn't even witty! A pig in a nightcap! When did a pig ever have a nightcap?

KOROBKIN (*continuing*): "The Superintendent of Schools reeks of onions from head to foot."

LUKA LUKICH (*to the* SPECTATORS): By God, I never had an onion in my mouth!

AMMOS FEDOROVICH (*aside*): Thank God, at least there's nothing about me!

KOROBKIN (*reading*): "The Judge . . ."

AMMOS FEDOROVICH: Now I'll catch it! . . . (*Aloud.*) Ladies and gentlemen, I think the letter's rather long. Devil take it, why read such trash?

LUKA LUKICH: No!

POSTMASTER: No, read it!

ARTEMY FILIPPOVICH: No, just read it!

KOROBKIN (*continuing*): "The Judge, Lyapkin-Tyapkin, is *movay tone* in the highest degree. . . ." (*Stopping.*) That must be a French word.

AMMOS FEDOROVICH: The devil knows what it means! It's all right if it's nothing but swindler, but it may mean something worse!

KOROBKIN (*continuing*): "But after all they're a hospitable and kind-hearted lot. Good-by, my dear Tryapichkin. I myself, following your example, want to become a writer. It's a bore to live like this, my boy; one needs food for one's soul. I see that exactly what I need is something lofty to occupy me. Write to me in Saratov Province, to the village of Podkatilovka." (*He turns over the letter and reads the address.*) "To Ivan Vasilyevich Tryapichkin, Esquire, Third Floor, Number Ninety-seven, turning to the right from the yard entrance, Post Office Street, St. Petersburg."

ONE OF THE LADIES: What an unexpected setback!

CHIEF OF POLICE: He's as good as cut my throat! I'm killed. I'm simply killed dead. I can see absolutely nothing in front of me but pigs' snouts instead of faces. . . . Get him back, get him back! (*He waves his arm.*)

POSTMASTER: How can we get him back? It's just my luck to have ordered the superintendent to give him the fastest horses; and the devil put me up to sending similar orders ahead.

KOROBKIN'S WIFE: This is certainly confusion worse confounded!

AMMOS FEDOROVICH: But, damn it, gentlemen, he borrowed three hundred rubles from me!

ARTEMY FILIPPOVICH: Three hundred from me, too.

POSTMASTER (*sighing*): Oh, and three hundred from me!

BOBCHINSKY: And from me and Petr Ivanovich, sixty-five, sir, in notes, yes, sir!

AMMOS FEDOROVICH (*shrugging his shoulders in perplexity*): How did this happen, gentlemen? How in the world did we make such a mistake?

Chief of Police (*striking his brow*): How could I, how could I, old blockhead that I am! Stupid old ram! I've outlived my good sense! . . . Thirty years I've been in the service; not a merchant, not a contractor has been able to impose on me; I've fooled swindlers upon swindlers; sharpers and rascals who could fool the whole world I have hooked neatly! I've bamboozled three governors! . . . What are governors! (*Waving his hand.*) Governors aren't worth mentioning!

Anna Andreyevna: But this can't be, Antosha; he's betrothed to Mashenka.

Chief of Police (*angrily*): Betrothed! A cat and a fiddle! Betrothed indeed! She dares to throw the engagement in my face! . . . (*In desperation.*) Here, just look—all the world, all Christianity, all of you—just see how the Police Chief has made a fool of himself! Blockhead that he is! the old blockhead, the old scoundrel! (*Threatening himself with his fist.*) Oh, you thick-nosed imbecile! To take a lounge-lizard, a rag, for a man of importance! And there he skims along the road with his bells jingling! He'll spread the story all over the earth! And I'll not only be a laughingstock, but some quill-driver, some paper-spoiler will be found to put me in a comedy! That's what hurts! He won't spare my rank or my calling; and they'll all show their teeth in a grin and clap their hands. What are you laughing at? You're laughing at yourselves! . . . Damn you! . . . (*He stamps on the floor in his rage.*) I'd like to do the same to all scribblers! Bah, you quill-drivers, you damned Liberals! You devil's brood! I'd like to tie you all in a knot and grind you to powder, and ram you into the devil's cap! . . . (*He strikes out with his fist and stamps on the floor. After a brief silence.*) I simply can't get over it. Indeed it's true that when God wants to punish a man, he takes away his reason first. Now, what was there in that weathercock like a government inspector? Absolutely nothing! Not even half a finger's length of resemblance; but suddenly everybody shouts, "The inspector, the government inspector!" Now, who was the first to let out the notion that he was the government inspector? Speak up!

Artemy Filippovich (*shrugging his shoulders*): I couldn't tell you how it happened if my life depended on it! It's as if a fog had descended upon us and the devil had misled us.

Ammos Fedorovich: Who started it? There's who: those two smart Alecks! (*Pointing to* Dobchinsky *and* Bobchinsky.)

Bobchinsky: Not at all! Not me! I never even thought . . .

Dobchinsky: I didn't do anything, absolutely not . . .

Artemy Filippovich: Of course you did.

LUKA LUKICH: It stands to reason. They ran in from the tavern like two lunatics, yelling: "He's come! He's come! and he doesn't pay anything! . . ." They found a rare bird!

CHIEF OF POLICE: Naturally, it was you. You town scandal-mongers, you damned liars!

ARTEMY FILIPPOVICH: May the devil take you with your inspectors and your yarns!

CHIEF OF POLICE: You just snoop about the town and mess things up, you damned chatterboxes! You scatter scandals, you bobtailed magpies!

AMMOS FEDOROVICH: You damned bunglers!

LUKA LUKICH: Dunces!

ARTEMY FILIPPOVICH: Pot-bellied little shrimps! (*They all surround them.*)

BOBCHINSKY: By God, it wasn't I, it was Petr Ivanovich!

DOBCHINSKY: It was not, Petr Ivanovich, you said it first. . . .

BOBCHINSKY: Certainly not; you were the first yourself.

LAST SCENE

The same and a GENDARME

GENDARME: The official who has come from Petersburg by imperial order demands your instant appearance before him. He is stopping at the inn.

(*The words just pronounced strike all like a thunderbolt. A sound of astonishment escapes from the lips of all the ladies at once; the whole group, having suddenly changed its position, remains as if petrified.*)

DUMB SHOW

The CHIEF OF POLICE *stands in the midst like a post, his arms outspread and his head tilted backwards; on the right his wife and his daughter appear on the verge of rushing towards him; beyond them the* POSTMASTER, *transformed into a question mark, is turned towards the spectators; beyond him* LUKA LUKICH, *in the most innocent bewilderment; beyond him, at the very edge of the scene, three lady guests are leaning towards each other with the most sarcastic expressions of countenance, aimed directly at the* POLICE CHIEF'S FAMILY. *On the* POLICE CHIEF'S *left stands* ZEMLYANIKA, *his head inclined somewhat to one side, as if he were listening to something; beyond him the* JUDGE, *with outspread arms, almost squatting on the floor, and making movements of the lips as if about to whistle or say, "So you see what you've come to, old lady!" Beyond him is* KOROBKIN, *turned towards the spectators, with one eye cocked and a derisive gesture toward the* CHIEF

OF POLICE; *beyond him, on the extreme side,* DOBCHINSKY *and* BOBCHINSKY *make movements of their hands towards each other, their mouths open, and regarding each other with bulging eyes. The other guests simply stand like statues. For nearly a minute and a half the group remains in this position.)*

THE CURTAIN FALLS